"Have I thanked you for he

Because it's all I can think

"I needed someone, and you were the only name in my head. After everything that happened between us, you never hesitated."

"Did you think I might?" Finn asked, a note of concern in his tone.

"No," she said instantly, and honestly. "But it still feels unbelievable. I owe you—"

"Don't worry about it."

Finn might not want to hear it, but she had things she needed to say.

"An apology."

"We don't need to talk about that right now."

Hayley swiveled on her seat to face him fully. "We should've talked about this a year ago, but I was a coward."

He shook his head, still not meeting her eye. "It's fine. It's in the past. What matters most now is that you knew you could come to me. I will find Gage. And you and I can visit as often as you want while we find the person who's been following you and hunting him."

INNOCENT WITNESS

JULIE ANNE LINDSEY

If you purchased this book without a cover you should be aware that this book is stolen property. It was reported as "unsold and destroyed" to the publisher, and neither the author nor the publisher has received any payment for this "stripped book."

Recycling programs for this product may not exist in your area.

ISBN-13: 978-1-335-59159-3

Innocent Witness

This is a work of fiction. Names, characters, places and incidents are either the product of the author's imagination or are used fictitiously. Any resemblance to actual persons, living or dead, businesses, companies, events or locales is entirely coincidental.

For questions and comments about the quality of this book, please contact us at CustomerService@Harlequin.com.

Harlequin Enterprises ULC
22 Adelaide St. West, 41st Floor
Toronto, Ontario M5H 4E3, Canada
www.Harlequin.com

Printed in Lithuania

Julie Anne Lindsey is an obsessive reader who was once torn between the love of her two favorite genres: toe-curling romance and chew-your-nails suspense. Now she gets to write both for Harlequin Intrigue. When she's not creating new worlds, Julie can be found carpooling her three kids around northeastern Ohio and plotting with her shamelessly enabling friends. Winner of the Daphne du Maurier Award for Excellence in Mystery/Suspense, Julie is a member of International Thriller Writers, Romance Writers of America and Sisters in Crime. Learn more about Julie and her books at julieannelindsey.com.

Books by Julie Anne Lindsey

Harlequin Intrigue

Beaumont Brothers Justice

Closing In On Clues
Always Watching
Innocent Witness

Heartland Heroes

SVU Surveillance
Protecting His Witness
Kentucky Crime Ring
Stay Hidden
Accidental Witness
To Catch a Killer

Visit the Author Profile page at Harlequin.com.

CAST OF CHARACTERS

Hayley Campbell—A Marshal's Bluff, North Carolina, social worker, formerly in love with Finn Beaumont, now in search of a missing teen.

Finn Beaumont—A Marshal's Bluff detective investigating the death of a local philanthropist. Still in love with his ex, Hayley Campbell, he'll stop at nothing to protect her, return the teen to safety and bring a killer into custody.

Dean Beaumont—A private investigator and brother to Finn, working hard to assist local law enforcement in locating the missing teen and arresting a killer.

Gage Myers—New to the foster care system following the untimely death of his parents, he's become an unintentional witness to a high-profile murder and is currently on the run.

Katherine Everett—A local philanthropist with a community center and homeless shelter project in development.

Chip Everett—Katherine's widower, who stands to inherit the empire, is a prime suspect in her death.

Chapter One

Hayley Campbell settled onto the bench at her usual picnic table and unpacked her lunch. The small park, nestled between the public library and social-services department, was her private oasis from 11:00 a.m. to noon, every Monday through Friday. The cooler of sandwiches and drinks at her side was a personal offering to anyone in need.

For Hayley, becoming a social worker had felt more like a calling than a choice, and she couldn't imagine doing anything else. Though at twenty-four, she still looked more like the average high schooler than a legitimate representative of the county. Occasionally, judges, lawyers and local law-enforcement officials tried to overlook her or not take her opinions as seriously as those of her older coworkers. It was an inclination she understood, but never indulged. She did her best to be a voice for the youth of Marshal's Bluff, North Carolina, and anyone else who needed to be heard.

Within a few minutes, a number of familiar faces began to arrive. She opened the large cooler at her side and continued her meal. Folks young and old made their way to her table, selected a drink and sandwich, then waved their goodbyes. She ate and read and watched closely for the one face she always hoped to see. Then, finally, he appeared.

"Hey, you," she said, brightening. She closed her book and set it aside as fourteen-year-old Gage Myers approached.

Composed of gangly limbs and one big heart, he took the seat across from her with a small grin. "Hey."

Gage had lost both his parents in a car accident the year before, and Hayley was assigned his case. Her heart had split wide open for him when she placed him into foster care. His parents had both been only children, and their parents were already deceased. Gage was one of many cases she'd never forget—she was sure of it. But he was something more too.

His olive skin was unusually ruddy as he watched her. His wide brown eyes, heavy-lidded. He looked as if he hadn't slept, but also as if he wanted to run.

Hayley shifted, suddenly nervous and hoping not to seem that way. A gust of wind tossed strands of stick-straight blond hair into her eyes. She tucked the locks behind her ear with care, using the small distraction to further evaluate her friend.

Gage's fingers and T-shirt were spattered with spray paint, a sign something had been on his mind. He used street art to work through the emotions too big to process with words. He'd been in trouble for defacing property more than once, but she'd never found it in her to be angry. His paintings were powerful, and it was a necessary outlet for the teen.

"You okay?" she asked finally, reaching to press the back of her hand against his forehead. "Are you getting sick?"

He rolled those big appreciative eyes up at her, the way he always did when she offered him comfort. "I think I saw something I shouldn't have," he said. "I don't really want to talk about it."

"Okay." She handed him a sandwich, a napkin and a drink. "You want to talk about something else?"

He shrugged and ate quickly, as if he hadn't in a while.

A growth spurt? She wondered. *Or hadn't he eaten breakfast? And if not, why?*

"How're the Michaelsons?" she asked, feigning casual as she fished for information. Gage's foster parents had never struck her as a good fit for the system. But they'd been housing children in need for more than a decade, caring for dozens of youths in that time, and they were one of the rare couples willing to host teenagers. Still, something always felt off when Hayley visited. Maybe Gage had witnessed something questionable there.

He shook his head, as if reading her mind. "It's not them this time." He sighed and glanced away.

She hated his clarification of "this time," but held her tongue, sensing there was more he wanted to say. But she intended to circle back. If there had been other times the Michaelsons were a problem, she needed to know.

Gage's lips parted, but he didn't speak. Something was stopping him.

"You know you can trust me, right?" she asked. "I will always have your best interests at heart, and I'd never take any action without keeping you in the loop. I'm here to be your advocate. Whatever you need."

She wished for the dozenth time that she could foster him, instead of the Michaelsons. Instead of anyone else. She'd try to adopt him if she thought the courts would consider it, but the system liked to see kids placed with couples, preferably married and stable ones. Ones who'd been out of college and in the workforce more than eighteen months, unlike Hayley.

His gaze lifted to something over her shoulder, and his

expression changed. He gathered the empty sandwich baggie and napkin from his vanquished lunch and stood. "I'd better go. Thank you for this." He wiggled the trash in his hands. "I needed it, and it was great."

"Wait." Hayley rose and removed another sandwich from the cooler. "Take this. And come back at five when I get off work," she said. "We can talk. If something's wrong at your foster home, you can stay with me while we straighten it out. Let me help you."

He nodded, eyes flicking to the distance again. "Yeah, all right."

She retook her seat. "All right," she echoed, swallowing the lump in her throat. She glanced over her shoulder, in the direction Gage had looked, but saw nothing of interest, then turned back to watch him go. Every fiber in her body urged her to chase after him, but she had no grounds to make him stay. "See you at five," she called, needing the confirmation.

He waved and nodded, then picked up the pace as he strode away.

THE AFTERNOON DRAGGED for Hayley as she attended a court hearing and made several home visits, checking on the other children in her caseload. At the office, she rushed through the paperwork, one eye on the clock and eager to take Gage somewhere safe so they could talk.

She was out the door at five-o'clock sharp, blinking against the bright southern summer sun. The air was thick and balmy, eighty-nine degrees with extreme humidity. The soft scents of sunblock and charcoal grills drifted by. Life in coastal North Carolina was beautiful at any time, but August was Hayley's favorite. She loved the extreme heat and the way everything was in bloom, lush and alive. Laughter carried on the wind, from parks and beaches, ice-cream parlors and outdoor cafés. She couldn't imagine living anywhere else, but she'd be a lot happier in the moment, once she knew Gage was okay.

At five thirty, she gave up the wait and began a slow walk to her car.

The social-services staff parked their cars in a series of spaces along the perimeter of a nearby church's lot. It was a protective measure against potentially unhappy clients, or family members of clients, who lashed out when court appointments didn't go the way they'd wanted. And it was an added level of privacy for workers.

In Hayley's experience, the people willing to destroy private property over a particular outcome probably weren't the ones who should have children in their care. But she also knew the system sometimes failed, and anyone could reach a breaking point when someone they loved was taken from them. She hoped to become part of the solution and a support for those in times of trouble.

She waited outside her car until six, then she called Mrs. Michaelson.

Gage's foster mom claimed she hadn't seen him since the night before, and she accused him of being on drugs before Hayley could get any useful information.

She rubbed her forehead as they disconnected. Gage was not on drugs. His eyes had been clear, if worry-filled, this morning. He'd been alert and on edge, not hung over.

Something else was wrong.

She climbed into her car and started the engine. She had a few ideas of where Gage could be. She'd had to search for him before, in the early days following his parents' deaths, when grief and despair had made him reckless and hostile. She hated to think of him feeling those ways again. Hated to think of him upset and alone.

The drive from Social Services, on the periphery of downtown Marshal's Bluff, to the fringe areas along the warehouse and shipping district was shockingly quick. The landscape changed in a matter of blocks, trading community parks and tree-lined streets for abandoned housing and condemned buildings.

To Gage's eyes, a neighborhood full of blank canvases for his art.

She slowed as small groups of people came into view, scanning each of their faces for Gage. Hayley noticed evidence of his artwork here and there, all older pieces she'd seen last fall.

After a trip around the block, she decided to go on foot, talk to folks, ask for help. She parked her sedan at the curb and climbed out, hyperaware that her pencil skirt and blouse stood out in ways that were unlikely to help her blend. She could thank her appearance in court for that. Typically, she wore jeans and a nice top. Outfits that made her more approachable to the people she helped. Less authoritarian.

Old Downtown was filled with buildings that blocked the bay views. Most were crumbling from age and in need of repair. Windows and doors were barred and boarded. No Trespassing signs were posted everywhere, so property owners wouldn't be sued if someone became injured while inside.

Hayley approached a group of young men on the stoop attached to a former barbershop and offered a small, hip-high wave. "I'm looking for a friend named Gage," she said. "Do you know him?"

The nearest kid, wearing baggy jeans and a long-sleeved flannel shirt, despite the heat, shot her a disbelieving look. "Who are you? His mom?"

Hayley shook her head, saddened by the thought. She'd give just about anything to bring Gage's mom back to him, or to have the honor of caring for him herself, but those things weren't options right now. And all that mattered was finding him and bringing him home safely. "I'm just a friend," she said. "He's about your age. He's an artist. He painted these." She lifted a finger to indicate a small black silhouette on one of the boarded windows.

Gage regularly used the image to depict children like himself, the ones he felt went unseen. Untethered numbers in case files. Kids nobody really knew.

"You know him?" the boy asked.

She bit her tongue against the obvious response. She'd made that clear, hadn't she? "Have you seen him?"

"Nah."

"Thanks." Hayley sighed and moved along.

"Hey," one of the other kids called to her, making her turn around. "Lady, I ain't trying to get in your business, but you shouldn't be down here. Nothing good is gonna find someone like you on this street."

"Noted," she said. "But I'm worried about my friend, and I need to know he's okay. If you see him, I hope you'll tell him I was here."

Dusk was settling, but she walked the neighborhood for nearly an hour as the sun lowered in the sky, eventually blunted by the buildings. She talked to knots and clusters of people along the way. Most were less friendly than the first group she'd encountered. Eventually, she was forced to call it a night, so she started back to her car.

The street was quieter on her return trip—the people she'd spoken to earlier were already gone. Her nerves coiled tightly at the realization she was alone. Wind off the water stirred loose sheets of newspaper and scooted empty plastic bags over broken asphalt, causing her to start and jump. Each sound and movement increased her already hurried pace.

When the breeze settled and silence returned, the echoing clicks of her high heels were offset by a softer, more distant sound of footfalls.

She beeped the locks open on her sedan and wrenched the door wide, tossing her purse onto the passenger seat. She slid behind the wheel with a sigh of relief.

In her rearview mirror, a shadow grew from the space between two buildings, stretching and morphing into the silhouette of a man. He moved pointedly across the street in her direction, barely ten yards away.

She waited, wondering if someone she'd spoken to earlier had something they wanted to tell her now.

Then he raised a gun.

Hayley started the car's engine and jerked the shifter into Drive as the first bullet ripped through the evening air, eliciting a scream from her core.

She peeled away as the second and third shots exploded behind her.

Chapter Two

Marshal's Bluff Detective Finn Beaumont collapsed onto his office chair and kicked his legs out in front of him. His head fell back, and he hooked one bent arm across his eyes. He was tired to his core, exhausted in ways he hadn't been in ages. And it was hot as blazes outside, where he'd spent most of his day, in a dress shirt and slacks, questioning socialites in swimming pools and executives on golf courses.

It'd been one of those days when he'd wondered if he really knew his town at all.

Katherine Everett, a local philanthropist known widely throughout the community simply as Kate, was officially missing. Kate's grandfather had established the largest shipping company in the area and grown it into a national conglomerate. Today, Everett Industries transported goods along both coasts and the gulf, as well as to countless inlet towns. Kate managed the family's estate and funneled her heart and soul into Marshal's Bluff rehabilitation efforts.

Everyone loved her, but she was gone. And after ten hours of interviewing her neighbors, family and friends, Finn was no closer to guessing her whereabouts than the moment he'd received the call this morning announcing her disappearance.

His appreciation for her work and love of his job were

just two of the many reasons he needed to find her fast. At twenty-five, he was both the newest and youngest detective on the force, and he had a lot to prove. When people with money went missing, and a ransom note didn't follow, foul play was a scary possibility. According to everyone he'd interviewed, Kate wasn't the sort to take off without letting someone know, and the calendars at her home and office showed a number of appointments happening all week. None had been canceled.

More bad signs.

The phone on Finn's desk rang, and he forced his head up, then stretched to lift the receiver. "Beaumont."

"Detective Beaumont," the desk clerk responded. "I have a social worker here who'd like to see you immediately. Possible missing child and gunshots fired in Old Downtown."

Finn rubbed his forehead. "Anyone hurt?"

"No, sir. Units are en route for follow-up."

He exhaled a long breath. He'd been on the clock nearly twelve hours, but sure. He'd see the social worker. "I guess there's always time for one more crisis, right?"

"That's the job," the clerk said, then disconnected the call.

A moment later, Finn heard the steady click-clack of high heels in the hallway.

He'd gotten nowhere while looking for Kate today, but maybe he could end the shift on a positive note by helping the social worker. He sat taller and straightened the files he'd slung onto his desk earlier, in a hurry to make his next set of interviews on time.

"Finn?"

His limbs froze, and his gaze snapped to his open office door. He'd know that voice anywhere, though he hadn't heard it in more than a year. "Hayley?"

Hayley Campbell had crashed into his life like a freight train during her first few weeks as a social worker. She'd faced off with some pretty rough-looking folks outside the courthouse when they didn't like the verdict about losing their children. He'd intervened before things escalated too far. And he'd asked her out the minute she'd stopped insisting she'd had the situation covered. Shockingly, she'd agreed.

The story of the whirlwind romance that followed was one he thought they'd tell their grandkids. But when he'd proposed a few months later, she said no. And she'd proceeded to ghost him until he stopped trying to reach her or make sense of her reaction.

He'd eventually let it go, but he wasn't over it. He doubted he ever would be. Life was like that sometimes, he supposed. People had to take the good with the bad. And the months he'd spent with Hayley were some of the best of his life.

Now, she stood before him in a pencil skirt and blouse that emphasized every dang curve on her petite little frame. Straight blond hair tucked behind her ears, she had a look on her face he knew all too well. Determination.

"Come in," he said, hoping to sound calmer than he felt. "Have a seat." The desk clerk's words rushed back to him with a slap. "You saw a shooter?"

He pulled a bottle of water from the nearby mini fridge and reassessed her expression when she didn't answer. Now, he could see she was doing all she could to hold herself together. "Talk to me, Hayley."

The sound of his voice seemed to pull her back to him, and she wet her lips. Unshed tears filled her blue eyes as she accepted the water and drank greedily.

Was she in shock?

He scanned her body more carefully, searching for signs of injury or physical trauma.

"I know it's not fair of me to come here like this," she said, voice shaky, "but I need help, and I don't want him to become another case ignored because he's been in trouble before. He hasn't run away. Either something happened to him, or he's hiding because he thinks something will happen."

Finn crossed his arms and sat on the edge of his desk before her. "Okay. I'm missing a lot of pieces, so let's start at the beginning. Who are you worried about? And when did you first know something was wrong? Take your time and be as specific as possible. Especially about this shooter."

She inhaled slowly, then released the breath and began talking about her lunch hour.

Finn took mental notes as she spoke, and a few literal ones on a pad of paper he scooped up, sticking with her as she carefully laid out the details of her day.

"When the first shot went off, I thought, maybe it was because I look like a person with money," she said, glancing at her modest skirt and sensible heels. "In that area, any amount of money is enough, you know?"

He nodded, tongue-tied as he imagined getting his hands on the person who'd taken a shot at his— Finn's brain halted and misfired. His what? Hayley wasn't his anything anymore. She hadn't been in a very long time. He cleared his throat and pushed ahead. "How many shots were fired?"

"Three. But by the second one, I was driving away. I don't think a robber would have persisted like that. I think this has something to do with Gage's disappearance. I called 911 on my way here, but I wasn't going to wait around for them. I needed to talk to you."

Finn's chest tightened at her final words. She'd avoided

him for a year, but when she needed help, she still looked to him. That had to count for something.

"All right." He pushed onto his feet and rounded the desk to his chair. "I need to get your official written statement and make a report. You can tell me all you know about… Gage, is it?"

She nodded. "Yes."

"I'll share his description and relevant information with Dispatch and let officers know he's missing, possibly in danger."

"Thank you." She released a long, steady breath. "What happens then?"

"Then I'll follow you home," he said. "It's unlikely the shooter will show up at your place, but an escort might make you feel better. It'll certainly help me."

HAYLEY SMILED, relieved and exhausted. Finn hadn't changed at all in the time they'd been apart. He was still kind and accepting. Still listened and didn't interrupt. And he still had her best interest at heart, even after she'd walked out on his proposal without an explanation. Then she'd hid from him, like a coward, for more than a year. "I'd appreciate it."

An hour later, she pulled into the driveway outside her cottage, several blocks from the bay, with Finn behind her.

Her neighborhood was a series of older homes packed closely together. The tiny yards spilled into one another all the way to the end of each block. It was a blue-collar, working-class section of town, established at the turn of the last century, when most of the male citizens worked on the docks or on ships in some capacity, hence its proximity to the sea. These days, however, her block had more retirees than worker bees. That fact had been a selling point on this property over all the others in her price range. The way

Hayley saw it, a block full of retirees likely meant someone was home all the time, which would keep crime low. Witnesses tended to ruin a criminal's day.

She grabbed her things from the passenger seat and climbed out, then met Finn on the porch. Hopefully, she hadn't left anything she'd regret Finn seeing in plain sight inside. She was tidy, but it'd been a while since she'd had company. An errant bra on the couch or coffee table wasn't unheard of at her place, mostly because removing the torture device was her go-to move after a long day at the office.

Hayley turned on the porch light as they entered. "I didn't expect to get back so late," she said, mostly out of nerves and habit. Finn used to worry about her returning to a dark home.

Her heart rate rose as they stood in the entryway between her living room and staircase to the second floor. The cottage suddenly felt smaller and warmer than she remembered.

She'd furnished the space in hand-me-downs and thrift-store finds, full of colors and textures that made her happy. Mismatched throw rugs and tables she'd saved from the curb on trash day, sanded and given new life with fresh paint.

"Can I get you a glass of sweet tea or a cup of coffee?" she asked.

He looked tired and a little anxious, but the second part couldn't be true. He was Finn Beaumont, a full six feet of handsomeness, with lean muscles, broad shoulders and two perfect, extra large hands.

She resisted the urge to pluck the fabric of her shirt away from her chest.

Her female coworkers always took an extra minute to

check their hair and refresh their lipstick before going to the police station or courthouse, just in case they'd see him.

"Sweet tea sounds nice," he said. "Thank you."

Hayley hustled into the kitchen, glad for the moment alone to collect her marbles. She poured a glass of tea from the pitcher she kept in her fridge, then straightened her skirt, took a deep breath and hurried back to the living room.

Finn stood at the fireplace, examining framed photographs on her mantel. She'd replaced the images of her and Finn with snapshots of children from her caseload, their artwork, or pics of her at community events and charity drives. The first photo he'd taken of her on the Beaumont ranch stood at the center of her collection.

The old wooden floorboards creaked as she moved in his direction.

"How's your mom?" he asked, casting a glance over his shoulder.

"She's fine," she said, passing him the glass.

Hayley didn't keep pictures of her mom, or talk about her, for a number of reasons. Her mother didn't bring her joy, peace or any of the other things Hayley needed her home to provide. And most of her memories involving the older woman upset her.

Finn scanned her briefly, then took a small sip of his tea. "You look nice. Were you in court today?"

"Yeah." She moved to the couch and Finn followed. "You look as if you've had a big day too."

He raised his eyebrows then laughed. "I have. But no one shot at me, so there's that."

She smiled.

"And even the worst days have bright spots," he added.

She sat and pulled a throw pillow onto her lap, hugging it to her chest. "How's your family doing? I recommend their ranch for rehabilitation every chance I get. I think some folks take me up on it."

Finn sipped the tea again before setting his glass on the coffee table. "I know my folks appreciate that." He rested his hands on his lap and grinned. "It's been a big year for the Beaumonts. Have you heard?"

She swiveled in his direction, curiosity piqued. "No. Do tell."

"Dean got back with his ex, Nicole. They're engaged now."

Hayley's heart swelled. She loved Dean, and knew he wasn't over his ex, but she'd expected him to move on, not find his way back to her. Did things like that really happen? "That's wonderful," she said, meaning it to her core. "Nicole has the younger sister who stayed at the ranch, right?"

"That's the one." Finn hooked one ankle over the opposite knee. "Nicole came to him for help when her sister went missing. They worked out their troubles, saved the sister and fell in love all over again. They're getting married in the spring."

Hayley pressed her lips together and felt her cheeks heat. The parallels between her situation with Finn and his brother's situation with his ex were hard to ignore. But she wasn't naive enough to think there'd be a way back to him for her. Not after what she'd done. Finn was kind and forgiving, but she'd gone too far.

"And then there's Austin," he began, a dimple sinking into his cheek at the appearance of his mischievous grin.

"What did Austin do?" She'd always liked Austin. He was the oldest of the biological Beaumont boys, third in line of the five, which actually made him a bit of a middle child and a goofball. Dean and Jake had been adopted as young boys, around the same time Austin and Lincoln were born only sixteen months apart. As a result, the brothers were close in every way and inseparable friends.

"He's currently engaged to a local real-estate agent," he said.

She shook her head in awe. "You're kidding?"

"Nope. He took her case when she thought someone was following her. She was right, and we handled that. Now Austin and Scarlet are planning a big Christmas wedding."

Hayley laughed. "I can't believe the Beaumont boys are getting married. Your mama must be elated. She's obsessed with seeing your family grow."

Finn's smile fell a bit, and reality knocked the awe from Hayley's tone.

"Oh—" She winced. "I didn't mean to—"

Finn had proposed long before Dean or Austin, but Hayley had said no.

He lifted a palm. "You had your reasons."

She had, but she also owed him an explanation. The words piled on her tongue, but wouldn't quite fall from her lips.

Silence stretched as he searched her eyes. "I suppose I should get going and let you rest," he said, the words low and thick. "I'll get a neighborhood patrol on your block tonight for good measure, and I'll keep you posted with any updates we have on Gage. You'll do the same?"

"Of course." She rose and walked Finn to the door.

"You still have my number?" he asked, pausing on her front porch.

She nodded.

His gaze flicked over her face once more. "For what it's worth, I'm glad you came to me," he said. "You can always ask me for help. Tomorrow or ten years from now. Won't matter."

She leaned against the doorjamb as her knees went a little weak.

"I mean it, Hayley. If you ever need anything, you can call me. Whether you're having a hard time and just want someone to listen, or you need a background check on your date. Maybe help opening a jar or reaching a high shelf."

She laughed. "Let me guess. You're my man?"

"I will always be your man," he said. Then he turned with a wink and jogged away.

Chapter Three

Hayley arrived at Social Services early the next morning. She hadn't slept well and decided to use the extra time to get ahead on paperwork. But the moment she'd taken a seat behind her desk, her mind was back on Gage.

A call to Mrs. Michaelson had confirmed his continued absence, which meant he was still missing and in trouble. He was a kid alone and on foot. And whatever he'd gotten into possibly involved a gunman.

She shivered at the memory of the silhouette as it had grown from the shadows. She wasn't sure she'd have survived if not for her car.

Gage didn't even have a cell phone.

By the time her coworkers began showing up, Hayley had already moved her laptop outside and set up a hot spot on her phone. If she worked at the picnic table where she ate lunch, it would reduce her chances of missing Gage if he stopped by to see her. Thankfully, her day's schedule was light. No court appearances, and only two home visits. She could keep a lookout from the park most of the day.

Sweat gathered on her brow and across the back of her neck as hours passed and the sun rose in the sky. She'd worn a blue silk sleeveless blouse with tan capri pants and flats. All in all, better suited for running than the prior day's pencil skirt and heels.

She'd struggled to choose between tops this morning and was mildly distressed by the outcome. She'd initially leaned toward a more figure-flattering cream blouse, but ultimately selected the blue because it matched her eyes. And Finn always used to comment when she wore blue.

The resulting internal cringe was nearly painful. She shouldn't be thinking about Finn Beaumont right now, or which color he'd liked on her a year ago. She should be focused on Gage and the gunman.

But since her mind had opened the Finn rabbit hole, she let herself tumble back down for another moment or two.

Two of his brothers were planning weddings. That was unexpected news. Dean never dated after Nicole broke his heart and Austin just never dated. Or, Hayley had never seen him with the same girl more than twice while she was with Finn anyway. Now, Dean had reunited with the woman he loved, and Austin had committed to a local real-estate agent. Whoever she was, she must be special. The Beaumonts certainly were.

Hayley loved the whole family and wanted them to be happy. She wished she could meet the women who'd stolen Austin and Dean's hearts. She wished she could attend the wedding ceremonies and celebrate with them. They were the brothers she'd never had. And now, she never would.

If only she'd been less broken and more understanding of her own damage at the time of Finn's proposal, she'd be part of his family now too. Instead, she'd done what she always did. She'd panicked and she'd run. She hadn't even seen the pattern until it was pointed out to her in therapy. She was working hard on correcting that kind of behavior these days. But until the proposal, she hadn't understood all the ways her emotional damage had shaped her entire life.

A cool breeze picked up, pulling her back to the moment.

She glanced around, wondering how long she'd been lost in thought. Then she opened her cooler and unpacked her lunch. The day was slipping away without any good news.

An hour later, she collected her things, ready for her two afternoon appointments.

A large black SUV pulled away from the curb across the street and moved slowly past the social-services building. The fine hairs along Hayley's arms and the back of her neck stood at attention as she watched it disappear around the corner. The vehicle was high-end and new, a familiar make and model, but she'd missed the license plate.

Thankfully, she didn't see the vehicle again all afternoon.

She returned to the picnic table at five o'clock and waited until six before leaving. She traded texts with Finn about the fact neither of them had news on Gage's whereabouts. And she fought the urge to go back to Old Downtown and overturn every brick until she found him.

At six, she began the slow trek to her car.

Intuition prickled across her skin as she scanned the world around her, feeling someone's gaze on her as she moved. She hoped it belonged to Gage.

Kids played in the park and coworkers chatted in the lot, but none paid any attention to her as she passed.

The dark SUV from lunch appeared at the curb across the street, and Hayley's steps faltered. This time, a man in a black T-shirt, jeans and a ball cap leaned against the hood, mirrored sunglasses covering his eyes.

She picked up the pace, wondering, belatedly, if she should've turned back to talk with her coworkers until the man left. But it was too late. Now, he'd know what she drove.

He crossed his arms and widened his stance, appearing to watch her as she unlocked her car door.

She pulled a flyer wedged beneath one windshield wiper into the car with her and locked the door. She raised her phone in the man's direction to snap a photo, but he turned away, then climbed behind the wheel of his SUV and merged smoothly into evening traffic.

A gush of relief rushed over her lips a moment before the three words scrawled across the paper came into view.

Leave This Alone

FINN PACED THE sidewalk outside the pub near the precinct. Hayley's message had been brief but pointed. She was leaving work and on her way to meet him. He'd suggested they chat over dinner, and she'd named the pub they used to frequent.

He'd walked straight out of his office and jogged the block and a half to wait for her.

Her navy blue sedan swung into the narrow parking area beside the pub a moment later, and she climbed out looking on edge.

He tried not to notice the way her pants clung to her narrow hips and trim thighs. Or how the blue of her blouse perfectly matched her eyes. But he couldn't stop the smile that formed at the sight of her sleek blond hair, pulled into the world's tiniest ponytail.

"You okay?" he asked as she reached his side.

"No."

Alarm shot through Finn's limbs as he opened the pub's door and waited while she stepped inside. A million reasons for her answer raced through his mind. None of them were good.

The hostess smiled. "Two?"

"Yeah. A booth if you have one," Finn said.

The young woman's gaze slid over Hayley. "Sure. Right this way."

She led them to a table in the corner and left them with a pair of menus.

Hayley sat near the window, leaving Finn the seat with a clear view of the door and room at large, which he appreciated. She frowned as she watched the hostess walk away. "I forgot what it was like to go anywhere with you."

"What do you mean?" He glanced around the busy pub, then back at her. Nothing seemed amiss. They'd passed several available tables on their way to this one, but his request had been strategic. "I thought a booth would give us more privacy."

She sighed and pulled a folded piece of paper from her purse, then passed it to him. "This was on my windshield when I left work, and I park at the church a block away from Social Services. That means whoever left it knew which car was mine. I'm afraid it might've been the same person who saw me drive away last night after they shot at me."

Finn raised his eyebrows. "You think the shooter wrote this?"

"I don't know," she said. "But a man was standing outside an SUV, watching me, when I found it. And I think I saw the same vehicle near the park at lunchtime. The guy left when I tried to take a picture of him."

"Did he look like the shooter?" Finn asked, blood pressure rising.

This wasn't the way he'd expected their exchange to go. Hayley hadn't mentioned any of this in her text. She'd just wanted to meet, and he'd assumed, at worst, she was still worried about Gage's absence. At best, he'd thought she might just want to see him again.

Hayley raised her narrow shoulders in an exaggerated

shrug. "I didn't get a good look at the person who followed me last night. All I know is Gage never went back to his foster home, and he didn't reach out to me today. I'm doing everything I can to find him, which for the record feels like nothing, and everything about my day was absurdly unremarkable until that appeared."

Finn read the note again. "You think this is a reference to Gage's situation?"

"What else could it be?" she asked. "Searching for him is the only thing I'm doing differently, and Gage said he thought he saw something he shouldn't. I'm guessing whoever is responsible for whatever he saw left this note."

Finn rested against the seat back, telling himself to remain calm and collected. He couldn't let his attachment to Hayley interfere with his ability to do his best work for her. "I'm going to need another formal statement," he said. "I'll put the note into evidence after we eat."

A waitress arrived with a notepad and a smile. "Are y'all ready to order?"

Finn watched Hayley for the answer, allowing her to decide. She hadn't even looked at the menu.

She slid her attention from the woman to Finn and pursed her lips. "Just a soda for me."

"And what can I get you?" the waitress asked, shifting one hip against the table and angling toward him as she spoke.

"You're not hungry?" Finn asked Hayley, confused. "Have you already eaten?"

"No. I'm just shaken."

"You have to eat." He looked at the waitress, who was smiling.

He frowned. "Can we get a basket of chicken tenders to split? Honey for dip. And I'll have black coffee."

"Sure thing, sugar. Anything else?"

"No."

The waitress left, and Hayley rolled her eyes.

"Did you want something different?" he asked.

She used to love chicken strips with honey. Had that changed this year?

She shook her head. "The order was good. Thank you. I'm just— What am I going to do?"

He waited, unsure how to answer without more specifics.

"I know this is bad," she said, pointing to the note he'd refolded and set aside. "I need to know how bad and what to do next."

"Well," Finn began, rubbing a hand along his jaw, "we'll need more information to answer the first part. Should we wait until you've had something to eat before we tackle the second? You look like you're ready to drop."

"No," she said. "And I am." She let her eyes close briefly and tipped her head over one shoulder.

Finn willed his gaze away from the exposed length of her neck.

Her lids opened and she straightened, fixing her attention on him. "I'm being followed by a man in an SUV who knows where I work and what I drive. Gage is still missing, and the man with the SUV doesn't want me looking for him, but I can't stop doing that. Gage's life could be in danger. Meanwhile there's a possibility this guy is the same person who shot at me. I feel sick."

Finn rested his forearms on the table between them and clasped his hands. Apparently they were going to talk about the tough stuff before eating. "You're right to be concerned about all that. I'm doing everything I can on my end to figure out what happened in Old Downtown last night. Officers walked the area you described but didn't find any evidence of the shooting. They're looking for the shell casings from the shots fired. If we find them, we can use ballistics to try to match the gun to other crimes and possibly get a lead on the shooter. I was running on the theory the shooting was a separate issue from the kid's disappearance, but the note makes this personal, and given the big picture, it's smart to proceed as if these things are related."

"Okay," she said softly, sounding frightened but in agreement. "Now what?"

"Now, I think it would be wise if someone looked after you for the next few days while we figure out what's going on here."

Her nose wrinkled. "Like a bodyguard?"

"More like a personal protection detail," he said. "I'll put a cruiser in your neighborhood and assign one to you at work. I'll fill in whenever I can so you're as comfortable as possible while being followed around."

Hayley blinked. "You're going to follow me around?"

"Just until we're sure you're safe."

The waitress returned with a tray and bent low to set it on the table, temporarily blocking his view of Hayley. "Chicken fingers with honey, black coffee and a soda," she said. "Is there anything else I can do for you?" She stood and cocked her hip again.

Finn followed Hayley's droll, heavy-lidded gaze to the smiling young woman. "No. This is everything. Thank you."

She left.

Hayley raised a chicken finger and pointed it at him. "That waitress is hitting on you. Just like the hostess. It's blatant and rude. We could be here together."

He furrowed his brow. "What?"

"You're an actual detective, Finn. You're literally paid to notice details, yet you are oblivious. How is that possible?"

Finn leaned forward, shamelessly enjoying her undivided attention and hint of possessiveness in her tone. "Probably because all I see right now is you."

A blush stole across her beautiful face, and she lowered the chicken. "Fine. You can follow me around, but you have to help me look for Gage too."

"Deal." He was already doing the latter, and he wanted the extra time with her.

She slid her hand over the table, fingers outstretched for a shake.

Finn curled his palm around hers and held tight, letting the intoxicating buzz of her touch course through him. "I will protect you," he promised. "And we'll find Gage. Together."

Chapter Four

Hayley rose with the sun the next morning. Unable to find sleep in more than small bits and patches during the night, she was glad to give up and get moving. She checked her phone with hope for missed news, preferably a message that Gage had been found, or a text directly from the teen saying he was safe. The only waiting notifications were social-media updates from coworkers and a few junk emails she marked as spam.

Disappointment washed over her, but not surprise. Nothing had ever come easily. At least, she supposed, this was familiar territory. Time to set a plan and get to work.

She hurried through her morning routine, dressing for the day and sending good thoughts into the universe, hoping the energy would find its way to Gage. Something to keep his chin up until she found him. And she would find him. Whatever it took. She wasn't sure she'd recover if something happened to the teen. He'd already experienced too much tragedy. He deserved a home filled with love and a safe place to exist while he grieved the loss of his parents. A place he could become the man he wanted to be without all the noise. Somewhere he could focus on his art and express himself freely.

Not on the run. Not alone and afraid.

She willed away the budding tears and pressed the brew button on her single-cup coffee maker. Then she packed a cooler of sandwiches, baggies of pretzels and cold water bottles while she finished her first cup. She returned the empty mug to the machine and brewed a refill.

Someone knew where Gage was. If she couldn't find him, she could at least find someone to point her in the right direction. All she needed was a lead.

Her thoughts circled back to the SUV outside her office and the note left on her windshield, then to the man with the gun. None of those things were clues to Gage's whereabouts, but they were all clues. She just had to figure out what they meant.

"What did you see, Gage?" she whispered, remembering his worried words to her at lunch, and hating that she hadn't been able to stop this, whatever it was, from happening.

Memories of the gunman sent a shiver down her spine, and she crept toward her front window for a careful peek outside. He knew her car and license-plate number, and her place of employment, so why not her address?

A familiar black pickup truck sat at the curb across the street. Finn was behind the wheel, a laptop balanced on something inside his cab as he typed away, stealing occasional glances into his mirrors and at her front door.

"Of course, you're already outside," she murmured, smiling as she rolled her eyes. "The Beaumont brothers and their big, dumb, hero hearts." She slipped onto her porch when he turned his attention back to his computer, then marched down her walkway in his direction.

As she drew nearer, it became clear he wasn't just starting work a little early. He'd been outside her place all night. He was wearing the same shirt from last night, and his usually clean-shaven face was dark with stubble. His hair pointed in all directions from one too many finger combs, and there was a level of fatigue in his eyes that only came from pulling an all-nighter.

He turned to face her before she reached the center of the street.

"Still got those heightened senses, I see."

He grinned, hooking one elbow through the open window. "Keeps me alive."

"Handy." She stopped at his door and lifted her chin to indicate the mess of empty snack wrappers at his side. "You want to come in for coffee, or are you full of jerky and candy?"

He climbed out and closed his door with a grin. "Coffee sounds amazing."

Hayley inhaled, steadying herself against his intoxicating nearness. Even after a night in his truck, his trademark mix of cologne and sea air seemed to cling to his clothes and skin. The inviting scent of his spearmint gum beckoned her closer. Heat from his body seemed to grip and pull her, as did his sleepy eyes and disheveled hair. Up close, Finn Beaumont was mesmerizing.

Memories of sleepless nights they'd once shared slid into mind, unbidden, raising her body temperature and heating her cheeks. She forced away the images and willed her heart and head to get a grip. Nothing about her bone-deep attraction and attachment to him would help her find Gage, and that sweet missing boy was all that mattered.

"Penny for your thoughts?" Finn asked, voice low and careful.

She shrugged, feigning confidence. "You could've stayed inside, you know. There wasn't any reason to sleep in your truck. I have a spare room."

He rubbed a hand against his stubbled cheek, looking

suddenly boyish and shy. "I'll keep that in mind. For now, I think all I need is a little coffee, and I'll be good to go."

She nodded and turned back to her home, leading the way across the street. "I'm asking a coworker to take some tasks off my plate today and tomorrow. I want to double down on my efforts to locate Gage before much more time passes. I'd hoped to get news during the night, but I haven't."

He nodded as she held open her front door for him. "If we don't make solid progress fast, I'll reach out to Dean and Austin, see if they can help."

Hayley's heart swelled. The duo owned a private-investigations office together, and they were very good. "Thank you."

"Of course. How much of your work were you able to off-load?"

"Most of it. I figure the less time I spend at the office, the less likely I'll be to draw a criminal stalker there. It's a building full of folks trying to make the world a little better for local kids and families. I can't be the reason something bad potentially comes into their lives."

"Always troubleshooting for others," he said with a small smile.

"That's the job."

"That's your heart," he corrected.

Hayley scanned his dark brown eyes. "Kind of like the way you insist on seeing the best in people."

She felt like a failure for not getting the whole story from Gage while he'd been right there at the picnic table with her. She'd failed when she let him walk away. Yet Finn managed to see her in the best light. As if she wasn't at least partially at fault.

"I can reach out to your supervisor," Finn suggested. "Let them know you're part of an ongoing investigation and that you'll be working with Marshal's Bluff PD outside the office for a few days."

"Not yet," she said. "I'm holding out hope that Gage will turn up soon and fill us in on what's happening. Then, I can take care of him while you arrest whoever is behind the gunshots."

She selected a mug from the cupboard and brewed him a cup of coffee, then passed it his way.

"Thanks." Finn accepted and blew over the steamy surface before taking a greedy gulp.

"You're welcome. Thank you for keeping an eye on me last night. Are you headed home to rest now, or are you on the clock for a bit longer?"

He lowered the cup slightly, eyebrows raised. "I've been off the clock since last night. Today's supposed to be my day off, but I'm in the middle of another case, so that was never happening. Why? What do you need?"

"I thought you might come with me to ask around about Gage, but I don't want to add more work for you on your day off." The people who roamed Old Downtown were unlikely to talk to a lawman, but at least some of the folks in Gage's world were likely to be motivated by a badge. His foster parents and siblings, for example. And Hayley could use all the help she could get.

Finn finished his coffee and set the mug on the counter. "Helping you will never be work, Hayley."

She blinked. Something in his tone suggested he might not be as angry with her for running away from his proposal as she'd imagined. That maybe he was over it. And not necessarily over her.

"Where do you want to start?" he asked, moving the mug to her sink for a rinse and allowing her to take the lead, despite a shiny detective badge on the leather bifold perpetually clipped to his pocket.

I'd like to start with a deeply apologetic kiss, she thought, but she pushed the silly notion aside.

"I was thinking I should go back to Old Downtown." Where she'd been shot at. Where her gut said Gage had been likely last seen.

"I'll drive."

FINN PARKED HIS pickup along the crumbling curb of Front Street in Old Downtown. The area was dreary, even by morning light. There would be more people around as the day commenced, but the danger increased with the population in this neighborhood, and Finn intended to keep Hayley as far away from trouble as possible. Meanwhile, they'd have to settle for questioning the early risers, typically an older, less hostile group.

Hayley swung open her door and climbed down, pulling a large black tote behind her. "Ready?" She closed the door without waiting for his response.

He met her at his back bumper and gave her a curious look. "What's with the luggage?"

He'd assumed it was her work or laptop bag when she'd carried it to his truck. Maybe she thought it would be stolen if she left it behind? "I've got a lockbox behind my seat, if you'd feel better leaving your things in there."

She smiled. "No thanks. I plan to give this away."

Finn frowned. "What?"

"I usually bring sandwiches and water to the office and distribute them at lunch. Folks know they can help themselves. Since I won't be there today, I thought I'd do what I can down here."

Finn opened his mouth to speak, but words failed. He'd

grown up in a family that made sure as many folks as possible had something to eat every day. His parents, particularly his mama, were still dedicated to the task. Since becoming a detective, he'd taken a much smaller role in the family's daily efforts, but seeing Hayley's considerate and giving nature in action melted him a little. He'd held out hope of getting over her one day, but clearly that wouldn't be today. Spending time with her on this case would set him back months in his quest to move on, but some sadistic part of him would enjoy the pain.

A woman wearing too many layers of clothing for the increasing heat and humidity appeared on the corner. She eyed him skeptically before taking note of Hayley at his side.

Hayley unzipped her bag and liberated a small bottle of water. She extended it in the woman's direction. "Going to be another hot one today."

The woman froze, but Hayley continued moving toward her.

"You can have this if you want it."

Finn slowed, hanging back to allow the women to interact.

"I have food too. If you're hungry," Hayley offered.

"What do you want for it?"

"Nothing." Hayley passed the water and a small pack of pretzels to the other woman.

"What are you doing down here?"

"I'm looking for the boy who makes those." She tipped her head to indicate a dark patch of graffiti, the silhouette of a child at the end of a long shadow. "He's my friend, and I haven't seen him in a couple days. I'm worried." She dug a sandwich from her sack and passed that to the woman as well. "If you need a place to stay tonight, somewhere cool and safe," she added, "the mission on Second Avenue has openings for women and children."

The woman's expression softened. "You're her, aren't you?"

"Who?" Hayley asked.

"The angel."

Hayley's eyes widened for a moment, but she rearranged her features quickly. Anyone who wasn't staring at her, like Finn was, probably wouldn't have noticed. "Pardon?"

The woman finished the water without answering. She tucked the sandwich into the pocket of her baggy cardigan. "I've got a place around the corner. I don't like the mission. It's too crowded, and there's a curfew."

"If you run into anyone who might need somewhere, will you let them know?" Hayley asked.

"Sure." The woman's gaze flickered back to the graffiti. "He's a nice kid," she said. "Seems right that he'd have someone like you." She lifted her eyes briefly to Finn, then moved away.

Hayley's expression fell with the woman's parting words, and Finn moved quickly to her side. "You all right?"

"Fine." She forced a tight smile. "Worried about Gage. That's all."

He wasn't convinced that was the whole story, but Finn knew better than to push her past her comfort zone. The last time he did that, she'd avoided him for a year.

They moved onward, searching for pedestrians to ask about Gage. Block by block, until her bag was empty. Everyone seemed to know the boy who painted the shadows of children. They were kind and concerned, but no one knew where he'd gone.

Finn's presence could easily have deterred folks from talking to her, but Hayley was just so genuine. Everyone could see it. The tough things she'd been through had somehow strengthened her instead of breaking her. She'd become stronger without becoming hardened. In truth, she was probably softer and more gentle-hearted as a result. People seemed to sense and respect that.

He set a hand on her back when they turned around at the waterfront.

Her narrow shoulders curved in defeat.

Regardless of how many people were willing to talk, Gage was still missing. Just like the heiress, Kate. And that was incredibly frustrating.

"Hey." The deep bass of a male voice turned them on their heels. A large man approached slowly from a nearby dock. He was tall and broad-shouldered with thickly muscled arms and deep-set brown eyes. He lifted his chin to Finn, then refocused on Hayley.

"Timothy!" Hayley moved quickly in the man's direction, meeting him halfway and smiling widely. "How are you? How's Sonia?"

Timothy's lips twitched as he seemed to be fighting a smile and he nodded. "All good, thanks to you. I heard you're looking for the little tagger."

"I am," she said, jerking her attention to Finn, then back to her friend. "He's missing, and I think he's in trouble. Have you seen him around here in the last day or two?"

"I try not to spend too much time out this way these days, but I heard you were here yesterday, and a friend told me why. I asked around for you." He balled one hand into a fist at his side, then stretched his fingers before letting them hang loose once more. "I encouraged folks to talk. I was just headed your way, to be honest. You shouldn't be down here. This place just ain't for you."

"You heard something?" she asked, ignoring his sage advice.

Finn glanced at Timothy's hand again and imagined it wouldn't take much effort on the mammoth's part to encourage anyone to do anything.

The man's steely gaze flicked to Finn. "What kind of law are you?"

"I'm with the Marshal's Bluff PD," Finn answered.

Hayley declared, "He's a friend."

Timothy rolled his shoulders and refocused on Hayley. "Some folks saw your boy at the rave a couple of nights ago. They noticed, because he was new, and he was running."

Hayley took a half step back, and Finn leaned forward to steady her.

"Running from who?" Finn asked.

"Don't know," the man said. "But more than one person saw him, so he was there."

"Where?"

"Winthrop's—you know it?"

"Yeah." The old warehouse had nearly burned down several years back. The owners couldn't afford the repairs, and their insurance had lapsed, so the city had condemned it. "That place isn't structurally sound. No one should be in there, especially not a crowd. The whole thing could've collapsed."

The guy made a painfully bland expression. "Not my business."

"Do you know when the next rave will be?" Finn asked. If ravers recognized Gage because he wasn't a regular, then maybe Finn and another detective could drop in and talk to attendees. Get firsthand information.

"Nah, man. It's a pop-up. Place changes. Day changes. Time changes. You know that, Detective." The last few words were said in a pointed tone, and Finn bristled. He hadn't told Timothy he was a detective, but he was right on both counts. Finn knew all about the raves. They were a thorn in the side of Marshal's Bluff PD. The department tried to bust up the parties anytime they could, but getting wind of one ahead of time had proven impossible, and hearing about a rave while it was in motion was rare. Lots of drugs and money exchanged hands on those nights, along with plenty of other illegal activities, he was sure. "Why'd you ask if I was a detective if you already knew?"

"That wasn't what I asked." Timothy turned dark eyes back to Hayley. "I asked what kind of law you are. She knew the answer."

Finn considered the words. Timothy had wanted to know if he could be trusted.

With that, the man turned and walked away.

Chapter Five

Hayley chewed her lip as she walked at Finn's side. She'd spoken to a lot of people in a short amount of time. No one had known where Gage was, but several women with children now planned to sleep at the mission, and more than a dozen souls weren't hungry at the moment, thanks to her trip to Old Downtown. Despite feelings of defeat, she couldn't be wholly disappointed in the morning's outcome.

She was especially thankful for Timothy's efforts to acquire information on the missing teen, though she hoped no one had been harmed in the process. Timothy's rage was legendary and the reason he'd lost his little girl to the system last year. The only thing bigger than his temper was his love for Sonia. So he'd taken the required anger-management courses, started working out and joined a local basketball league to burn off the excess stress of his job and being a single parent. He'd gotten Sonia back in only a few months. He did the work and set a good example for his daughter. Hayley had endless respect for that. And sincere appreciation for the lead he'd provided on Gage, thin as it was.

"I know the rave has been over for days," she said, stealing a look at Finn. "But Winthrop's is only two blocks from here."

He slid his eyes to her without missing a step. "You want to go there?"

She nodded. "I know Gage isn't there, and likely no one else will be either, but it's all we've got to go on right now. If we leave without stopping by, I'll wonder if we missed a huge clue, and it will eat at me."

Finn inhaled deeply and released the breath on a slow exhale. "I'd rather send a couple of uniforms to follow up on that, but I don't suppose that'll satisfy you?"

Hayley stopped walking. "It's the only place I know he's been in the last couple of days, aside from visiting me at lunch. I need to see it."

She was certain every protective fiber in Finn's body wanted to get her away from Old Downtown as quickly as possible, but he knew her well enough to understand she wasn't asking his permission. Letting her go alone was more dangerous than going with her, so he'd agree eventually. "Come with me?"

A long, quiet moment elapsed between them. A muscle in his jaw flexed and tightened. Then, he cracked. First his expression, then his stance. "Fine, but I go in first, and you stay with me. Not just where I can see you, but within arm's reach. That place was condemned for a reason. It's unsafe. And it's known to attract trouble."

"Agreed." Hayley turned and headed in the direction of the old warehouse that overlooked the harbor. She concentrated to keep her steps even, though she wanted to break into a run. As if Gage might be there if she hurried. Instead, she slowed her breathing, reminding herself to be vigilant and focused. She had no idea what she might find if she really looked.

Finn increased his pace casually when they got closer to the building, his long strides forcing her to speed up. He placed himself a half step ahead on the sidewalk outside the door, then raised one arm in front of her like a gate.

Hayley stilled, surveying the crumbling, neglected exterior. Winthrop's was a stout, vacant space that had once held boats and shipping containers for the fishing company. The property, formerly home to a thriving enterprise, was now a heinous eyesore. Its charred bricks and cracked windows rotted darkly beneath a scorched metal roof. All evidence of the fire that had bankrupted the owners.

Finn opened the door with little effort, and she followed him inside—they were as silent as two ghosts.

The air was hot and dry, laced with salt from the nearby ocean and ash from the singed interior beams. Litter covered the floor—empty liquor bottles and beer cans, fast-food wrappers and cigarette butts. Ironic, she thought, to smoke in a building that'd nearly burned to the ground.

Finn moved methodically through the space, examining the open areas, then clearing the sections blocked from view by partial walls and pallets of materials from an abandoned reconstruction effort.

Distant sounds of the ocean, bleating tugboats and screaming gulls, traveled in through a large portion of missing wall at the back. Hayley moved to the floor's edge and peered over the steep plummet to the water. Intense sunlight reflected off the crystal surface, while small white wave breaks rolled steadily toward the shore. The drop from the warehouse was survivable, if the unfortunate person landed far enough away to hit the water, or close enough to begin an early roll down the hillside, instead of a midpoint smack against the narrow, rocky shoreline below.

Thankfully there wasn't any sign of Gage, hurt, suffering, or worse, in view.

She imagined him running through the warehouse packed

with people and music raging into the rafters, then leaping to his escape.

"You okay?" Finn asked, moving to her side.

"Yeah." She pulled her gaze away from the water, blinking to refocus on him in the shadow of the building. "Notice anything useful?"

He shook his head. "You want to walk the perimeter?"

She led the way back through the front door and around the side of the building. Her skin heated with the late morning sun as they moved over broken asphalt. Humidity tugged at her hair and added beads of sweat to her temples.

When they'd finished the circuit, Finn turned to her, hands on hips. His frown suggested he was as frustrated as she was. "I'm sorry this didn't go better."

"It's not your fault," she said, feeling the pressure of defeat on her chest once more. "At least everyone around here knows I'm looking for him. Someone will deliver the message."

Finn nodded, his keen gaze and trained eyes dragging over everything in sight, probably seeing a lot more than she did in the dirty streets and dilapidated landscape. "I'm in the middle of a missing-persons case too," he said, surprising her with the unexpected disclosure. "I was looking for her all day yesterday and hoping for a win today. I'm not used to striking out twice in a row."

Hayley had no doubt that was true, but she kept the thought to herself. Beaumont men rarely failed at anything they were determined to achieve. "Who were you looking for?" she asked. "I'm sure they'll turn up with you on the case."

She offered a small smile he didn't return.

"Katherine Everett."

"The philanthropist?" she asked, officially stunned.

"Yep."

Hayley raised her eyebrows. "Any chance she'll turn up at a spa retreat in the mountains?"

"So far, she doesn't seem to be anywhere."

"Did you know she's building a shelter and community center down here?" Hayley asked. "She wants to make better use of all these blocks of crime and waste."

"I've heard," he said. "My family's ranch donated to the effort. It's long overdue. People experiencing homelessness should have somewhere safe to stay while getting on their feet."

Hayley's heart swelled at his words. It was easy to forget how steeped in this community Finn and his family were, and that his parents dedicated themselves to the betterment of life for Marshal's Bluff youths. "It's hard enough for people to find themselves in need of shelter. Harder still when the only placement available is in the basement of an old church—not that staying at the mission isn't better than being on the street," she clarified.

"There's a lot to be said for dignity," Finn agreed. "The entire project will add hope to an area that's been without it too long. This town has too many people in need. Kate's project will be an incredible boon."

"It will," she agreed. "The number of kids in our local foster system is beginning to outweigh the number of available families. I don't suppose you've thought of adopting?" Hayley asked.

When she'd dated Finn, he'd talked about wanting children of his own, but he'd make a great role model for any child. He was tough but fair, strong-willed but willing to compromise and loving but never a pushover. All things that struggling youths needed in their lives. For their emotional security and as an example of what a leader and high-quality human should be. "Or maybe becoming a foster parent?"

Finn pursed his lips. "I work too many hours. Kids need routine and reliability, not an adult running off at all hours, or one who's never home for dinner." He dragged emotion-filled eyes back to her. "If I had someone to care for, I'd want them to know they could count on me to be there."

Hayley tucked a swath of windblown hair behind her ear, his searing gaze burning a hole in her heart.

"How about you?" he asked. "Have you considered fostering or adoption?"

"I wanted to foster Gage," she confessed. "I knew the moment I met him. I could be there for him, helping in any way he needed. I could make him feel seen and loved. Support him through his grief. But I also know the system prefers couples and people twice my age for foster families, so I didn't bother throwing my hat in the ring."

Finn frowned. "What happened with him? How'd he end up on your caseload?"

"He lost his parents last year. A drunk driver. Before that, the three of them were a run-of-the-mill, happy family."

Breath left Finn in an audible whoosh. "Oh, man. To go from that to the system—"

"Yeah."

"No relatives?"

"None." Though Hayley certainly felt as if Gage was her family, and she wished she would've asked to foster him when she had the chance. She should've pleaded her case. But at the time, she'd felt the way Finn had described, unsure she had time to be all the things Gage needed. She was gone ten hours a day and often brought her work home. Plus, she'd never been a parent. She had no experience raising a teen, and she'd been a teen not so long ago in the court's eyes. She wasn't sure she'd ever actually been a kid, though. She'd been taking care of herself and her alcoholic mother since she could reach the doorknob to let herself in and out for school and trips to buy bread and eggs. "I didn't try to get him placed into my care, because I knew there'd be a fight in court. I'd have to prove myself, and I didn't want him drawn into all that when he'd just been orphaned. It wasn't fair."

"Most things aren't," Finn replied. "But you're the one out here looking for him now. What about the family he was placed with, what are they doing?"

Hayley bit back a barrage of unkind thoughts about the Michaelsons. "They have several kids at their place. I'm sure they're doing their best."

Finn narrowed his eyes. "Yeah?"

She looked away. The Michaelsons weren't her favorite foster family, but they seemed to do what they could, and that was more than she could say for some.

"I'm just learning Gage's story, and so far I know you're the one feeding him lunch every day. You're the one he came to see when something was wrong. You know about his art, and there's pride in your eyes when you look at it. Even though you know defacing public property is a crime. I'd say the two of you have chosen one another, regardless of the court's decision. You should see what you can do about that after we find him."

Hayley blinked back tears at the perfection of his words and the sincerity in the delivery. "He's a good kid. He shouldn't be painting the buildings, but he's not hurting anything down here, and he's working through his stuff." She scanned their surroundings in search of Gage's work and spotted an example several buildings away. Finn was right. She was proud of the kid's talent, and his outlet of choice. Plenty of other young adults in his situation would lash out with violence or fall into drug use. Gage chose to send messages to others who felt unseen, and to the system that made them feel that way.

She moved toward the painting in slow motion, drawn by something she couldn't put a finger on.

"What do you see?" Finn asked, falling into step at her side.

"It's unfinished." She lifted a finger to the silhouette when she noticed the missing section. "Why would he leave it like that?"

Finn examined the place where the image ended abruptly. "Out of paint?" he mused.

Hayley spotted a can on the ground across the street and went to pick it up. She gave the cylinder a shake then pointed the nozzle at the ground and pressed. A thick stream of black emerged.

Finn grunted. "We're not far from the rave location. He said he saw something he shouldn't?"

She turned slowly, following his train of thought. "He could've been standing across the street, painting, when something went wrong. Then he ran."

"Raves are nice and loud," Finn said. "Plenty of people and chaos. Easy place to disappear."

And Winthrop's warehouse had a giant escape hatch in back.

A spike of adrenaline shot through her. She was likely standing where Gage had been when he'd seen the thing that scared him. If she was right, then she knew what he'd been doing and where he'd run to hide. "What did he see?"

She scanned the area with new eyes, searching all the places and things visible from her standpoint. An apparition of heat rolled like fog above the street. The rising sun baked her fair skin.

Finn rubbed the back of his neck. “With a rave going on nearby, there would’ve been a lot of witnesses if something happened on the street. I’d guess he saw something done discreetly, through a window or in an alley.”

“It’s not uncommon for people to keep their mouths shut about crime,” Hayley said. “No one wants to get involved or become a snitch.”

“But Gage ran,” Finn countered. “He’d had a safe and normal life last year. So the question becomes, did he run explicitly out of fear, or because he was being chased?”

“Chased,” Hayley said, suddenly confident in her answer. “Why run through the rave if not? And why was the can over here, when he was painting across the street, and the rave was down there?”

Finn looked from Hayley to the incomplete artwork, then down the block to Winthrop’s warehouse. “The can could’ve been kicked or blown over—” Finn’s words stopped short, and his gaze fixed on something.

“What is it?” Hayley asked, moving closer to watch and listen.

“My gut,” he said. “See the big orange *Xs* painted on those doors?”

She followed his line of sight to the set of buildings in question. All were in rough shape, but none appeared any worse than the other structures around them. “It means they’re marked for demolition.”

“They’re being razed for Kate’s project,” Finn added. “She purchased a large section of adjoining properties. Construction won’t begin until next year, but removal of everything in the work zone starts in a few weeks. I read up on all the details after she went missing." He turned to Hayley, eyes wary. "Kate disappeared two nights ago."

"The same night Gage saw something." Hayley considered the unlikely possibility that her friend's disappearance could have anything to do with a wealthy philanthropist. "Kate wouldn't have any reason to visit this place at night, would she?" Or at all? Didn't investors only show up when their projects were complete? To cut a ribbon with giant scissors and make a public speech?

Finn took a step toward the nearest building with a big, orange *X*. He bumped her as he passed. "We might as well take a look around while we're here."

"You don't think the two are connected?"

He tipped his head noncommittally, left then right. "Probably not, but I like to cover my bases."

Hayley stepped aside when they reached the door, allowing Finn to try the knob.

Her heart rate climbed as the barrier creaked open. A wall of heat and sour air sent them back a step.

Finn covered his mouth and nose with the collar of his shirt, while she fought the urge to gag. "Stay here."

Hayley easily complied, angling her face away, desperate for the fresher air.

A low guttural moan and series of cuss words rose from the detective inside. He crouched over a still form covered in newspapers and raised a cell phone to his ear. "We've got a crime scene," he said.

"Is that…?" Hayley asked.

He glanced remorsefully in her direction. "Yeah." He stretched upright and returned to the doorway. "This is Detective Finn Beaumont," he told the person on the other end of his call. “I need the coroner and a CSI team with complete discretion. No lights or sirens. Unmarked vehicles. I’ve just found the body of Katherine Everett.”

Chapter Six

Hayley leaned against a telephone pole on the sidewalk near Gage's unfinished painting while men and women swarmed the street, working the crime scene. The first responders on-site wore plain clothes, as Finn had requested. Those who came later had on ball caps and T-shirts with the Marshal's Bluff PD logo, or the simple black polos of the coroner's office. A handful, presently taking photographs, setting up small, numbered teepees, or swabbing the building for trace evidence, wore lanyards and carried toolboxes with *CSI* emblazoned on them.

Hayley used the massive wooden pole at her back for support and concentrated on her breathing. She didn't need a criminal-justice degree to know what Gage had seen that night. And how much trouble he was in now. There'd be a large bounty on the head of the person who killed Katherine Everett, beloved community member and philanthropist. She and her family's money single-handedly funded two seasonal soup kitchens, kept the lights on at the mission's shelter for women and children and made sure no Marshal's Bluff student left school on weekends, holidays or summer breaks without food. Her family had the means to hunt down anyone with information about her murder. Making Gage a major liability to the killer.

Understanding why anyone would want to harm her was another story.

The coroner had declared the cause of death as blunt-force trauma. The weapon, a broken two-by-four, had done irreparable damage to her skull and brain. The bullet in her chest was unnecessary excess.

A commotion at the opposite curb drew Hayley's attention to a news van, the first of what would undoubtedly be many within the hour. Thankfully, Kate's body was long gone, removed from the crime scene by the coroner as quickly as possible following his arrival. There'd been a brief exam, preliminary findings were recorded, then she was loaded into the van and taken away. The media wouldn't get the salacious photos they hoped for today.

Officers met the crew as they climbed out, directing them to relocate behind the barricades a block away.

Yep, Hayley thought. *Chaos is coming.*

An unmistakable thrumming drew her eyes to the sky, where a helicopter appeared, bearing the local television station's call number in bright red.

Word was definitely out now.

A sharp whistle turned her around and raised an unexpected smile on her lips.

Austin and Dean Beaumont appeared. They strode in her direction, long legs eating up the distance to her side.

Austin lifted her off the ground in a hug, and Dean embraced her the moment his little brother set her free. They smiled broadly, offering warm greetings and reminding her of another reason she'd loved being in Finn's life. His brothers were the very best.

"We just heard about this," Dean said, blue eyes flashing with interest. "We were hired to take the missing-persons case this morning."

"Barely started our research before the call came," Austin added. "This is messed up."

"Agreed," Hayley said.

Dean scanned the bustling scene, then shot the chopper a death stare. "She was a huge proponent of good things here. I can't understand who'd do this."

"That makes two of us," Hayley said.

"Three," Austin countered. "How much do you know?"

Hayley exchanged information with the brothers, falling easily into the familiar rapport. Austin was a Beaumont by blood. Dean and his younger brother, Jake, an ATF agent, had been adopted as kids, not that it mattered, or anyone ever talked about it. Still, in her line of work, and with her heart set on gaining custody of Gage, it warmed her to know families could blend and heal into one perfect unit when enough love and dedication was involved. She had both in spades.

Austin folded his arms, taking in the scene. "You think your missing kid saw what happened?"

She nodded and pointed to the unfinished painting. "I think he was painting when he saw her murder, or the killer leaving the scene, and ran."

Dean scrubbed a hand through thick, dark hair and swore. "That'd put a target on his back. Whoever killed Kate will know her family has the money and connections necessary to find them."

Austin's gaze traveled thoughtfully over the silhouette painted on the nearby building. "Your kid painted this?"

Hayley nodded, pride filling her chest.

"He's good."

"He is," she agreed.

Gage's potential to heal from his unthinkable losses and become a man who made a difference in the world was outstanding. Even if he felt lost sometimes, Hayley could see the warm, bright future out there waiting for him. And she'd stick by him until he saw it too.

"I've noticed these shadow people popping up around here for a few months," Austin said. "I wondered who was responsible." He turned an appreciative look her way. "I'm impressed the artist is just a kid."

Hayley swallowed the lump in her throat. "He's a good kid who's had a bad year, and he doesn't deserve any of this."

Dean gave Hayley a pat on her back, then headed across the street toward Finn.

Austin watched him go, then squinted appraisingly at Hayley.

Goose bumps rose on her skin. It was already unfair that Beaumont men were so disarmingly attractive, but the fact they also seemed to share some kind of mind-reading ability was just too much. She rolled her eyes. "What?"

"Long time no see. Where ya been hiding, Campbell?"

She looked away, in no kind of headspace for the conversation he wanted.

"Okay," he relented, breaking into a ridiculously breathtaking smile. "I get it. We can talk about what happened between you and my brother another time."

"I'm literally never talking to you about that," she said sweetly. "Ever."

"Wrong."

Hayley laughed despite herself. "Goof."

Finn's pain had no doubt affected everyone who loved him. She was sorry about that, but there was only one person she'd discuss her failed relationship with, and it was Finn, not Austin.

"I know some people out this way," he said, changing the subject. "I'll put out some feelers and see what I can learn about your boy. One thing that's always true in this business is that nothing goes completely unseen. If my informants can't dig him up, or won't tell me where he is, I can at least ask them to keep him safe until we find whoever's responsible for this." He tipped his head toward the building where Kate's body had been found.

Unexpected emotion stung her eyes and blurred her vision. The idea strangers might look out for Gage until she could do the job herself pulled her heartstrings. Renegade tears rolled over her cheeks, and she swiped them away.

"Hey now." Austin stepped forward, pulling her against his chest and wrapping her in a hug. He rubbed her back in small, awkward strokes. "We'll find him and bring him back to you safely. That's a promise."

Hayley returned his embrace, holding on tight to her would-have-been brother-in-law and to a thousand silent prayers that he was right.

FINN'S GAZE DRIFTED past Dean's shoulder, drawn to Hayley yet again. He couldn't quite believe she'd dropped back into his life after a year of silence, or that she was really standing across the street right now. Had they actually spent the day together? And how was she so wholly unaffected by their split, when it had broken him completely?

They'd been in love. He'd proposed, and she'd vanished.

The memory still gutted him, but he was glad to see she was doing well. Even at his worst, he'd hated the possibility she was sad or alone. He'd had a horde of family members to comfort and annoy him during the tough times. Hayley didn't have that.

Across the street, Austin's smile faded and he embraced her. Hayley held him tight.

"What do you suppose that's about?" Dean asked.

"It's been a day," Finn answered honestly. And it was barely afternoon. "I'm sure she needed it."

"We all miss her, ya know?" Dean asked.

"I know."

Hayley fit with his family in ways he never dreamed someone could. She belonged with them, if not with him. And he hoped that maybe, after this case was closed, she'd come around more often. She didn't have to be lonely when there was an army of Beaumonts who loved her. If she wanted them, he'd even keep himself in check so she wouldn't feel as if their presence in her life required his.

"You ever find out what happened with her?" Dean asked.

"Why she loved me one minute and disappeared on me the next?" Finn squinted against the southern summer sun. "Nope. And I don't plan on it. If she wants me to know, she'll tell me."

"Funny she didn't call the police about the gunman or her missing kid," Dean said, his tone painfully casual.

Finn frowned. "She came directly to the station."

Dean nodded, keen gaze darting back across the street to Hayley and Finn. "Most people get shot at, they call 911."

"And?"

"She drove straight to you."

Finn widened his stance and crossed his arms over his chest. "Because she's smart."

Dean grinned.

"I plan to find her missing kid as soon as possible," Finn said. "Likely before we figure out who's after him. I'd like to set him up at the ranch until I'm sure he'll be safe elsewhere. I can't promise he won't run again if we take him back to the foster home, and Hayley will want to keep him with her if he doesn't stay there."

"That'd put her in danger," Dean said.

"Exactly. Any idea how many beds are open at the ranch right now?"

"No, but there's always room for one more," Dean said, quoting their mama. "I'll let her know he's coming when I drop in for dinner."

Finn nodded his gratitude. "He paints those."

Dean followed his raised finger to the painting behind Hayley and Finn. "She mentioned that. Kid's got talent."

"And a heart for people. Probably one of the reasons Hayley bonded with him so quickly."

"He'll be a good fit at the ranch," Dean said. "Lincoln can show him the ropes. Redirect his energies. Give him another outlet while this is sorted."

"Good idea. Lincoln could use a project involving people." Their brother, a recent veteran and current stable hand, spent too much time alone, brooding, with the animals. "He'd be feral by now, if not for Josi."

Dean puffed air through his nose. "I don't know how she puts up with him, but they make it work."

Finn couldn't help wondering how long they'd continue to make it work after Lincoln realized he was in love with the young stable manager, but that answer would come in time.

"Heads up," Dean said, pulling Finn's attention to Hayley and Austin.

The pair headed across the street.

Hayley appeared unsure, as if she might be asked to vacate the crime scene, even with the three of them at her side. Austin looked as he always did, entitled to be anywhere he pleased.

"Hey there, brother," Austin said, offering Finn the quick two-step handshake they'd adopted in high school. "Your girl caught me up on things. Now, what's our move?"

Finn ignored the pinch in his chest at Austin's word choice, then turned to the beauty at his side. "I think it's time to let your office know you'll be out for a few more days. Until we identify Katherine Everett's killer, we'll need a revised plan for your safety."

Hayley nodded. "Okay."

And Finn would start by accepting that spare bedroom she'd mentioned this morning.

Chapter Seven

Hayley curled on her couch that night with a bottle of water and take-out tacos. She and Finn had left the crime scene shortly after his brothers' arrival, and she'd tagged along when Finn was called to the station. A few hours later, they'd picked up dinner. Nothing about her day seemed real. In fact, she'd spent the past twenty-four hours feeling as if she was trapped in a terrible dream. Gage's fear. His disappearance. The gunman. Now a dead socialite. None of it made any sense.

Still, the truth sat two cushions away, unwrapping his third El Guaco Taco. The urge to poke Finn with a finger, just to make sure she wasn't dreaming, circled in her thoughts. Her one true love, and almost-fiancé, was at her home after a year of silence between them, and planning to sleep over. For her protection. Was any of this even real?

"Ow." Finn turned amused eyes on her. "What was that for?"

She bent the finger she'd poked him with and returned the hand to her lap. "Making sure I'm awake," she admitted. "This day has me questioning everything."

"Well, I appreciate the offer to stay in the spare room," he said, running a paper napkin over his lips. "The truck isn't as comfortable as it looks."

Hayley laughed, surprising herself and earning a grin from Finn.

He gathered their discarded wrappers when they finished, then headed for her kitchen.

"You don't have to clean up," she called, twisting to watch him over the back of the couch as he walked away.

"And you didn't have to let me stay here, but you did." He retook his seat a moment later, a little closer to her this time.

"Do you really think someone might show up here?" she asked, images of the man outside the black SUV flashing through her mind.

Finn offered a small, encouraging smile. "I don't want you to worry, so consider this a favor to me. I always assume the worst where criminals are concerned, and in a worst-case scenario, I can do a much better job protecting you from in here than from outside. Plus, this gives me peace of mind, which means I might get some sleep. I need the rest if I'm going to find Gage and capture Kate's killer as soon as possible."

Hayley relaxed by a fraction. "Have I thanked you for helping me? Because it's all I can think about. I needed someone, and you were the only name in my head. After everything that happened between us, you never hesitated."

"Did you think I might?" he asked, a note of concern in his tone.

"No," she said instantly, and honestly. "But it still feels unbelievable. I owe you—"

"Ten bucks for tacos?" he asked, shifting forward and taking his gaze with him. "Don't worry about it."

Finn might not want to hear it, but she had things she needed to say.

"An apology."

"We don't need to talk about that right now."

"Finn." Hayley swiveled on her seat to face him fully. "We should've talked about this a year ago, but I was a coward."

He shook his head, still not meeting her eye. "It's fine. It's in the past. What matters most now is that you knew you could come to me. I will find Gage, and Dean's talked to our folks. Gage can stay at the ranch until we know he's safe. They're already making room. You and I can visit as often as you want while we find the person who's been following you and hunting him."

Hayley's heart swelled at Finn's casual use of the word *we*. He wasn't pulling the detective card or shoving her away. He certainly had every right, especially when he hadn't let her apologize or explain why she'd vanished on him last year. He deserved so much better.

Finn's phone rang and his lips twitched with the hint of a smile as he looked at the display. He lifted a finger to Hayley, indicating he needed a moment before he answered.

An immediate and nonsensical stroke of displeasure coursed through her. Was he seeing someone? Did she care? She certainly had no right.

"Hey, Mama," he said. "Everything okay?"

Hayley grabbed her water bottle for a long drink, then worked to get her head on straight. She wasn't the jealous type, and she had no claim to Finn. Clearly, all the turmoil from a wild day had scrambled her brain.

"Which channel?" he asked, pulling Hayley's attention to him once more.

She grabbed the television remote and passed it his way.

"Thanks, Mama. Love you." He disconnected the call and navigated to the local news. "They're covering Kate's case on Channel Three."

"I saw the chopper this morning."

"Yeah," he said. "I guess they sent a crew later."

Finn leaned forward, resting his elbows on his thighs as he waited.

Two overly charismatic anchors announced the next segment, and Finn pumped up the volume.

Soon the streets of Old Downtown appeared. Words scrolled across the bottom of the screen announcing "Death of a Philanthropist: Body of Katherine Everett located among trash in abandoned building."

"She was covered in newspapers," Finn complained. "It was meant to disguise the body as a sleeping squatter. They make it sound as if she was tossed beside a pile of garbage bags, or worse. The media always has to sensationalize everything." He kneaded together his hands, visibly annoyed. "They do this junk intentionally for views, and it gets the public all wound up. Then the phone lines at the station are bombarded for a week with citizens worried about a million nonemergency, nonthreatening things."

Hayley tucked her feet beneath her and focused on the television. She knew exactly what he meant. Anytime something bad happened in town, the local news blew it up as big as they could and anxiety rose across the board. Social workers, counselors and medical professionals all saw corresponding rises in their workload for as long as the secondary situation continued being covered.

On the TV screen, a reporter stood outside the building where Kate's body had been found. The sun was low in the sky, the CSI team gone, as she gave the most generic of comments about the day's events.

"This is good," Finn said. "Sounds as if we've kept a lid on the details." The relief in his features touched Hayley's heart.

Finn gave his all in everything he did.

He'd done a lot of very nice things with her once.

She shook away the sudden rush of heat and memories as the camera angle changed, widening to reveal a familiar face at the reporter's side. "A local private detective, Austin Beaumont, has been at the scene all day."

Finn groaned. "This explains why Mama was watching the news. He must've told her he'd be on."

"Why didn't he tell you?" Hayley asked.

The look on Finn's face suggested he could think of a number of reasons his brother hadn't mentioned the on-screen interview, and none of them were great.

"Can you tell us what brought you to Old Downtown today?" the reporter asked. "Were you hired to assist in the investigation of Katherine Everett's murder? Was it Marshal's Bluff PD who reached out to you, or was it a private party?"

Austin sucked his teeth and stared at the camera. "At Beaumont Investigations, we take privacy seriously, and we don't answer questions." He tipped two fingers to the brim of his hat and walked away.

Hayley burst into laughter.

Finn smiled as he watched her. "I thought that was going to go much more poorly. He hates reporters."

"Well, he's smart," she said. "He parlayed that annoyance into excellent business exposure."

Finn lifted the remote, whether to turn the television off or the volume down, she wasn't sure, but her breath caught as a familiar figure and dark SUV appeared on-screen. "What's wrong?" he asked.

Hayley blinked, afraid the man might disappear if she looked away. "I think that's the guy I saw outside the parking lot when I found the note."

Finn paused the television before the scene could change. Then he lifted his phone once more.

A mass of chills ran down Hayley's spine, and a slight tremor began in her hands.

"Ball cap. Sunglasses. Black T-shirt," Finn said to someone on the phone. He pointed the remote toward her television again and the SUV rolled off-screen.

"Dammit," Finn said. "They didn't catch the plate." He wrapped up his call and turned to her. "How do you feel about staying at my place?"

"Not great," she said honestly. "I'm hoping Gage will realize he needs help and come here to find me."

Finn leveled her with his trademark no-nonsense stare. "I understand that, but I can protect you better there."

She dithered, frozen by an impossible choice. How could she risk missing Gage? But how could she know he'd come? If he didn't seek her, and she or Finn were injured as a result of waiting for him, it would be her fault. If she left and Gage was injured after arriving and not finding the help he needed, it would be her fault.

"I can assign someone to keep an eye on the house," Finn said gently. "If Gage comes here, they'll intercept him."

Her heart dropped at the possibility Gage would come to her home for help, and she wouldn't be there.

"I have a guest room too," he reminded her. "It's not the same as sleeping in your own bed, but at least you'll know you aren't in danger."

"I'm not sure I'll be able to rest anywhere tonight," she admitted.

Not with Finn under the same roof.

"What if I remind you that the minute my mama knows you're there she'll be on her way with casseroles and hugs? All shameless ploys to keep you."

Hayley thought of Mrs. Beaumont's warm hugs and casseroles, then pushed onto her feet. Everyone would be safer if she agreed to Finn's terms, and that was all that mattered. "Who can say no to your mama's casseroles?"

"No one yet."

"I guess I'd better get dressed and pack a bag," she said, heading swiftly toward the stairs.

"Mama wins again."

FINN DROVE SLOWLY to his place, watching carefully for signs of a tail. He'd been concerned twice in town, but as the traffic and bustle of Marshal's Bluff gave way to rural back roads lined with farms and livestock, his truck quickly became the only vehicle in sight.

Dean and Austin were already in place. They'd swept the property and posted up as additional eyes to verify Finn and Hayley arrived safely.

The home had been purchased under the name of a limited-liability corporation to increase anonymity. And he'd spent several long weekends outfitting the place with abundant security measures.

Still, an influx of misplaced dread tightened his gut as they drew nearer. The last time Hayley had visited Finn's home, he'd proposed. He'd spent hours preparing that day, lining the driveway and drenching the sprawling trees in twinkle lights. Even longer practicing what he would say. The weight of the engagement ring in his pocket had felt life-affirming. He'd known without a doubt that the woman at his side was meant for him, and he would've done everything in his power to make her happy. Forever.

An hour later, she'd been gone. And his phone hadn't stopped ringing for days as the news swept through his family.

"I forgot how beautiful this place is," Hayley said, pulling him back to the moment.

Security lighting illuminated his home and perimeter landscaping now. Hidden cameras tracked and reported everything to a system inside. Silhouettes of his brothers' parked vehicles came into view at the back of the home as the driveway snaked around an incline.

Two familiar figures moved into view, hands raised in greeting as Finn drove the final few yards.

"Looks like we're all clear," he said, glancing her way.

Hayley's smile was radiant. "I'm always amazed by how intimidating this couple of goofballs can appear."

Finn shifted the truck into Park and considered his approaching brothers once more, trying to see them from someone else's perspective.

They were tall and broad, moving in near sync with long, determined strides. Their expressions were hidden beneath the shadows of plain black ball caps. He supposed, at first glance, or if he squinted a little, he could imagine them as dangerous. But anytime he saw Austin and Dean working together like this, he could only think of the time they'd attempted to build a tree house, only to wind up in a fight over the design that rolled them both off the platform.

Finn climbed out to thank their personal protection detail. They exchanged greetings and farewells, then Finn grabbed Hayley's bags and led her into his home.

He watched from the window as his brothers' taillights shrank in the distance—but he knew they wouldn't go far. Dean and Austin would likely split up and take shifts. One keeping watch on Finn's home, the other running leads on Gage's whereabouts. Like Finn, the PIs wouldn't get much sleep until this was over.

"I'll take your things to the guest room," Finn said, turning back to Hayley. "Make yourself at home. Consider this place yours until it's safe for you to go home."

"Thank you."

Finn moved through the open-concept living space and kitchen to a hallway with three bedrooms and a shared bath. His throat tightened as he fought a wave of unexpected and unpleasant emotions. Now wasn't the time to get nostalgic or wish things had gone differently. They hadn't. And that was life.

"Wow," Hayley said, her voice carrying to his ears. "You've completely remodeled."

He opened the guest-room door and set her bags on the bed, allowing himself one long breath before squaring his shoulders and heading back. "Yeah."

He'd taken his excess energy out on his home following their breakup, starting with refaced cabinets, new countertops and a farmhouse sink in the kitchen. Refinished floors, new paint and light fixtures everywhere else. He'd barely had a day off in the last year that hadn't involved at least one trip to the local hardware store.

"It's great," she said. "I love it."

"Thanks." Finn emerged from the hallway to find her admiring the kitchen. "Can I get you something to drink?"

She shook her head and her cheeks darkened.

He told himself she wasn't thinking of the things they'd done on his old countertop, and he pushed the thoughts from his mind as well.

"I should probably try to sleep," she said.

"Of course. I've got some work to do so…" He let his eyes fall shut when she passed him, making the trip to her room, not his.

THE SOUND OF the doorbell shot Finn onto his feet the next morning. He stumbled back, knocking his calves against the couch and blinking away the remnants of sleep he hadn't meant to get. A bevy of curses ran through his thoughts as he moved forward, wiping his eyes and hoping to stop the bell from chiming again.

A rush of breath left his chest as he passed the front window. A familiar truck was parked beyond the porch. He checked his watch, then opened the door.

His parents waited outside, smiling brightly as the barrier swung wide.

"Morning, Mama," he said, planting a kiss on her head as she hustled past.

"Morning, baby boy," she cooed, already halfway to the kitchen. She'd tied her salt-and-pepper hair away from her face in a low ponytail and wore jeans with boots and a T-shirt. Oven mitts covered her hands, a foil-covered casserole in her grip.

Finn was still wearing the sweatpants and T-shirt he'd changed into before beginning his online research the night before.

"Dad." He drew the older man into a quick hug, then followed him to the new granite-topped island.

"Morning."

Finn dragged a hand through sleep-mussed hair and rubbed fatigue from his eyes. "Can't say I'm surprised to see y'all, but you could've waited until at least eight."

"We've been up since five thirty," his dad said, adjusting the cowboy hat on his head. His black T-shirt was new and emblazoned with the ranch insignia. His jeans and boots were probably from the year he'd gotten married. "Your mama's been trying to get me out the door since six."

Mrs. Beaumont tucked the casserole into Finn's oven and set the timer. "He came up with every chore under the sun to do before we could leave."

"That's the life of a farmer," his dad said, setting additional dishes and bags onto the counter. "Can't be helped."

"We have farm hands," she countered. "You were stalling."

"You were rushing."

Mama shrugged and turned her eyes to Finn. "Where is Hayley? Can we see her?"

"She's not a puppy," his father said. "And she's probably still in bed. It's barely seven a.m."

"Nonsense. Who's sleeping at this hour?"

Finn raised a hand. "I was sleeping until you rang the bell."

"Silly." His mama fixed him with a no-nonsense stare. "It's time to start your day. We've heard all about what's going on. It was smart of you to bring Hayley here. She's much safer in our hands than alone at her place."

Finn traded a look with their father. His mother's use of the word *our* implied that she planned to stay involved. Probably not the best idea, but there was little to be done about it. No one talked her out of anything. Ever.

"We fixed up the storage cabin for the missing boy. Gage, is it?" she asked. "He'll like it. Tell me about him."

Soft footfalls turned all their heads to the hallway, where Hayley appeared. Her pink cotton sleep shorts and white tank top were slightly askew. As if she'd hurried out of bed without thought of straightening them. Emotion crumpled her features. "Morning, Mama," she said, voice cracking.

"Sweet girl," his mama said, a moment before engulfing her in a hug.

A lump formed in Finn's throat as his father welcomed her back too.

Working this case without getting his heart broken again in the process was quickly disappearing as an option.

Chapter Eight

Hayley sank into the Beaumonts' welcoming arms. Though she prided herself on her fierce independence, there was something about a group hug from good parents, even if they weren't hers, that made everything better. Mr. and Mrs. Beaumont treated the entire world like family. They'd cared for her emotionally since the day they'd met, celebrating her victories, asking about her troubles and supporting her silently when she just needed to be in the presence of someone who truly saw her. She'd missed them horribly for the past year, but the weight of their absence hadn't fully hit until now.

She wiped her eyes discreetly as the couple pulled away. Then she smiled through tears of joy. "It's so nice to see you again."

"We brought food," Mrs. Beaumont said, batting away a few renegade tears. "There's a casserole warming in the oven, and I prepared some sandwiches, potato salad, fruit salad and a cheese-and-cracker assortment for later. There's a lasagna in the freezer, and a pie in the fridge."

A bubble of laughter broke on Hayley's lips. She looked to Finn, and found him smiling as well. The expression sent a jolt of warmth through her core.

Mr. Beaumont carried a pile of plates to the island, arranging one before each stool. Finn poured coffee into four mugs, and their fearless matriarch bustled cheerfully, preparing for the meal.

This could have been Hayley's life.

Every day.

But she'd let fear and unhealed trauma take that from her, and it was too late to get it back.

Hayley shoved aside past regrets and focused on the present. "Did I hear you say you've made room for Gage at the ranch?"

Mr. and Mrs. Beaumont turned to her, pride in their nearly matching expressions.

"We did," Mr. Beaumont said. "We turned one of the small storage cabins into a private space for him. He'll have plenty of room for independence and privacy while still being a stone's throw from us." He turned a thumb back and forth between his wife and himself. "Lincoln will work with him until he finds his rhythm."

Mrs. Beaumont's expression melted into concern. "Is that okay? We haven't overstepped?"

Hayley refreshed her smile, realizing it had begun to droop. "No. Of course not. The cabin sounds perfect. Thank you."

Finn moved in her direction and set a hand between her shoulder blades. "Gage is very important to Hayley," he said, giving voice to her thoughts when her tongue became wholly tied.

She dropped her gaze to the floor. "I should've fought for the ability to foster him the moment we met. I should be the one caring for him."

"You are." Finn spread his fingers and pressed gently against her back, offering the reassurance she craved.

When she raised her eyes to his, electricity crackled in the air.

Mr. Beaumont cleared his throat, breaking the strange spell. He exchanged a look with his wife. “We know quite a few people in positions to help you when the time comes. You can count on that.”

Hayley’s bottom lip quivered, and she nodded, unable to speak once more.

The Beaumonts had strong ties to everyone in the courthouse and offices related to child and family services. Their ranch was a major player in the rehabilitation and healing of youths. If anyone had the ability to influence related outcomes, it was them.

“Here, sweet girl,” Mrs. Beaumont said, approaching and separating Hayley from Finn. “Let me feed you. Then you can tell us all about the boy who stole your heart.”

Hayley’s traitorous gaze moved to Finn and back to his mother, who’d caught the slip.

Mrs. Beaumont added scoops of casserole and warm, sliced bread to their plates. His father served fruit salad, and Finn delivered the caffeine.

Together, they took their seats and dug in.

Hayley told the Beaumonts all she knew and loved about Gage. Then she shared the little she’d learned about his disappearance. The older couple listened carefully. When the plates were mostly empty, Hayley’s heart and stomach full, Mrs. Beaumont turned serious eyes on her son.

“Tell me what you know about Kate’s death,” she directed Finn.

He caught her up quickly, then refilled everyone’s mugs.

“It’s a real shame,” his mother said. “Kate was a special woman. Her heart for this town and its citizens was huge.

She was smart in business and driven by her compassion. I can't imagine who'd want to stop her."

"Was it a robbery?" his dad asked.

Finn shook his head. "Unlikely. She didn't have a purse or identification on her, which could point to a mugging, except that she was still wearing a watch and necklace with a combined value higher than my annual salary. And someone covered her in newspapers. Could've been a sign of regret as much as an attempt to disguise the body. The missing purse was possibly a failed attempt to misdirect the police or hide her identity."

"Any suspects?" Mrs. Beaumont asked.

"None that stand out for now," Finn said, taking a long pull on his coffee. "Finding our young witness will be a major help."

Hayley chewed her lip, reminded again that Gage was in hiding, alone and scared.

"I've got plans to interview the husband and some workers from the charity," Finn said. "We'll visit Gage's foster family while we're out, see if we can make some progress on that end as well."

"I doubt they know anything," Hayley said. "If he'd gone back there, someone would've called me."

"Speaking to the other foster kids could be useful," Finn said. "When I was young, I told my brothers everything."

"Still do," his mother said, looking slightly affronted. "Luckily, I've got a sixth sense for when something is going on with my kids, and I can usually press the weak link for information."

"For the record, I was never the weak link," Finn declared, one palm against his chest.

Hayley smiled, falling easily into rhythm with the family she'd always wanted. The family she could've had.

If she hadn't panicked and blown it.

FINN PILOTED HIS truck into the Michaelsons' driveway an hour later. His parents had hurried away after breakfast to handle business on the ranch, and Hayley had gotten ready quickly for a new day of investigation.

Despite the heat, she'd chosen jeans that stopped mid-calf, sneakers and a blue silk tank top that accentuated her eyes and her curves.

"Here we go," she said, climbing down from the cab.

Finn met her at the front of his truck and reached for her hand. She accepted easily, and he squeezed her fingers before releasing her to lead the way to the door.

The old clapboard home was gray from age and weather. The red front door was battered with dents and dings. An array of toys and children's bikes cluttered the overgrown front lawn and walkway. All in all, it wasn't an idyllic scene, but Finn tried not to judge.

"How many kids are living here?" he asked, scrutinizing the postage-stamp yard and modest home.

"Five," Hayley said. "There are three bedrooms. Three middle-schoolers in one. Gage and a younger boy in another. Mr. and Mrs. Michaelson in the last."

Finn stared into the overflowing trash receptacle as Hayley rang the bell. Beer bottles were visible inside the bags. He had no problem with enjoying a drink or two, but there were more than a few visible bottles.

The door swept open before Finn could point out his concerns.

A woman in her late forties blinked against the sun. Her wide brown eyes were tired, her frame thin and shoulders curved. "Miss Campbell?" the woman asked, clearly stunned to see Hayley, though the disappearance of a child in her care should've made this meeting obvious and inevitable.

"Hello, Stacy," Hayley said. "May we come in?"

The woman stepped onto the porch, pulling her door shut behind her. "Sorry. Everyone is still sleeping. Can we talk here?"

Hayley's eyes darted to the closed door and back. She forced a tight smile. "Of course. This is my friend, Detective Beaumont. We're here to talk to you about Gage."

The woman looked at Finn, skin paling. "I'm not sure what you mean."

Finn flashed his badge, blank cop expression in place. "Can you tell us anything more about his disappearance? Have you heard from him? Any idea where he might've gone?"

She wrapped her arms around her middle, thin dark hair floating above her shoulders in the wind. A T-shirt and jeans hung from her gaunt frame, and heavy makeup circled her eyes. "Gage hasn't been home in a while now. I've asked everyone and searched everywhere but no one has seen him. Teenagers are like that. Always running off and disappearing. Probably one of the reasons it's so hard to find families who will take kids his age."

Hayley's jaw dropped, and Finn pressed a palm discreetly against her back.

"Ma'am, I'm quite familiar with teens and young people who struggle," he said. "I grew up at the Beaumont ranch, have you heard of it?"

She worked her jaw. "Sure."

"I've spent a lifetime in this arena, and in my experience, kids come home when they can. Assuming this is a safe place offering food, shelter and welcoming arms."

"Of course, it is." She tutted and slid her eyes to Hayley. "We offer all those things here."

Finn straightened to his full height, drawing the other woman's attention once more. "In that case, we have to ask what's stopped him from being here these past couple of nights. And every answer I can think of is reason for your concern, not contempt."

"Couple of nights?" Mrs. Michaelson raised an eyebrow. "That kid has barely bothered to spend more than a few hours at a time here in weeks."

"Weeks!" Hayley yipped. "What do you mean? How is that even possible?"

Mrs. Michaelson shrugged. "I told you—teens like their space. I can hardly help it if Gage won't stick around."

Finn opened his mouth to speak, but Hayley beat him to it.

"Why haven't you reported him missing?" Hayley demanded. "Or as a runaway?"

"He's a teen," Mrs. Michaelson said dryly. "They come and go. Besides, he always comes back eventually."

A little gasping sound leaped from Hayley's mouth. Her pointer finger flew up, and Finn grabbed it, covering her entire tiny fist with his.

He gave a small shake of his head when she struggled. "Ms. Campbell has lunch regularly with Gage and had no prior knowledge that there was a problem here."

"Guess he had you fooled too," the woman sneered.

Finn released Hayley and widened his stance, catching Mrs. Michaelson with his most pointed gaze. "You've continued to receive and deposit payments from the state for his full-time care, though you've only seen him a few hours at a time?"

The smug expression slowly bled from her face.

Hayley stiffened. "If you can't be bothered to report one of the children in your care as missing, it's clearly time for a thorough review of your status as a foster family. I'm guessing no children should be staying here."

"Well, good luck finding anyone to take in these teens. Besides, it sounds as if you're the one who dropped the ball on Gage. Not us." She ducked back inside and pulled the door shut hard behind her.

Hayley made a deep sound low in her throat. She turned and stormed up the walkway toward Finn's truck, towing him along by the hand.

Finn spun Hayley to face him when they reached the passenger side door. The tears in her eyes tore through his heart like talons. "Hey," he whispered, stealing a look at the home before pulling Hayley against his chest with ease. "This isn't your fault. She's in the wrong and trying to project that back on you. Her anger and accusations were redirects. Nothing more." He ran the backs of his fingers gently along her cheek, then tucked a swath of hair behind her ear. "We'll figure this out. Together. Okay?"

She nodded and wiped away a stream of falling teardrops. "Okay."

A red playground ball rolled into view from behind a patch of hedges, and a dirty-faced kid crept out to grab it. He startled when he saw Finn and Hayley watching. "My ball," he said in explanation, moving slowly to retrieve the toy. "I'm not supposed to play out front."

Finn's gaze jerked to the home and back to the boy. "You live with the Michaelsons?"

He nodded.

So much for everyone being asleep, as Mrs. Michaelson had said.

"I'm Finn. What's your name?"

"Parker."

Hayley crouched before him, immediately bringing herself to the child's height. "Hi, Parker. I'm Hayley. Do you remember me?"

Another nod.

"Have you seen Gage lately?" she asked.

"No." The boy wet his lips and dared a look over one shoulder to the home at his back. "But he always comes back for me."

Finn's muscles tightened as he imagined all the reasons a teenage boy would come back for a kid who was no older than eight. "He took care of you when he was here?"

"Yes, sir."

Hayley glanced at Finn in alarm. "How did Gage take care of you?"

The kid hugged his ball but didn't speak.

"You can tell me anything," Hayley promised. "I won't tell the Michaelsons, and if you're unhappy here, I can help you with that."

Something Finn suspected was hope flashed in the boy's eyes.

"Gage shared his food when we got some, and he gave me water when we had to play outside all day. It gets hot. Sometimes we aren't allowed to go in, and I get a headache."

Hayley raised a hand to her mouth, but dropped it quickly away. "Gage is a great kid. So are you. I'm not surprised you're such good friends. Did he help you with anything else?"

"He told us all stories when the grown-ups fought."

"Do they fight a lot?" she asked.

Parker looked at his ball.

Finn considered that a big yes.

"Do you have any idea where Gage is now?" Hayley asked. "We're trying to find him and make sure he's okay."

"I think he went home," Parker whispered.

"Where's—" Finn's words were cut short when Parker suddenly stiffened, turned and ran away.

He darted into the trees along the lawn's edge as the front door opened, and Mrs. Michaelson stepped outside.

"What are you still doing here?" she yelled. "You can't just hang around on my property!"

Finn felt the anger vibrating from Hayley's small frame and opened the passenger door to usher her inside. "We'll sort this out with the courts," he said quietly. "Meanwhile, let's go before we stir up a bees' nest and possibly make things tougher for the kids."

He closed her door and rounded the hood, keeping one eye on the angry woman in the distance. When he climbed into the cab, Hayley was on her cell phone.

"We need a wellness check at 1318 Sandpiper Lane," she told whoever was on the other end of the line. "I'd also like to request a full and comprehensive review of the Michaelsons."

Finn shifted into gear and pulled onto the street with a grin. It sounded as if smug Mrs. Michaelson was the one to open that can of worms, and Hayley Campbell was going to make her eat them.

The cell phone in his pocket began to ring as Hayley finished her call. Austin's number appeared on the dashboard console.

Finn tapped the screen to answer. "Hey, I've got you on speaker. I'm in the truck with Hayley."

"I'm glad you're together," Austin said. "I swung by Hayley's place, and it looks as if someone's inside. Since it's not you, I'm assuming it's a break-in. Things look secure from the front. They must've used a back door or a side window to enter."

Hayley dropped her cell phone to her lap. "Someone's inside my house?"

"Yep," Austin said. "I saw a light go on behind the curtain."

Finn took the next right, setting a course to Hayley's home. "Have you called it in?"

"Kind of what I'm doing now, Detective," Austin drawled.

Finn cast a look at Hayley's worried face, then returned his attention to the road. "Keep watch. We're on our way."

Chapter Nine

Hayley's muscles tensed as she processed the situation. She shifted and slid on the bench seat as Finn took a final wild turn into her neighborhood. "How long has Austin been watching my house?"

"Since last night. He and Dean have been taking shifts since they left my place."

Panic warred with appreciation in her chest as the truck roared onto her street, then entered her driveway.

Austin's truck stood empty at the end of the block.

Finn unlatched his seat belt and set a hand on the butt of his gun.

"What are you doing?" she whispered, curling nervous fingers around Finn's wrist before he attempted to leave her behind. "Shouldn't you text Austin to see where he is? Or call for backup?"

Finn gave her a pointed stare, and she released him. "I need you to wait here. Lock the doors. Keep your phone at the ready. I'll check the house and report back."

Hayley reached for her door's handle, then she climbed out of the cab.

Finn hurried after her. "What are you doing?" he hissed, speeding around the hood to meet her.

"I'm not waiting alone out here like a sitting duck," she

said. "I'll take my chances with whatever is going on in there. Right beside a trained lawman with a gun."

Finn pursed his lips but didn't argue. He tipped his head toward the front door, and she nodded.

Hayley moved along behind him, attempting to mimic his strides and posture, hoping not to alert the intruder to their presence. She crept up her front steps, then followed his example as he pressed his back to the wall near her door. On the opposite side of her porch, the front window curtain shifted.

Finn raised a closed fist, indicating she should wait.

This time she didn't protest.

The distinct clattering of dishes in the kitchen set her heart to a sprint as Finn reached for the front doorknob.

The door swung open before his fingers made contact.

Hayley's breaths stopped as she sent up a flurry of silent prayers.

Finn cussed and holstered his weapon. "What are you doing?"

"Eating, man." Austin poked his head and shoulders over the threshold, looking both ways before grinning at her. "Hey, Hayley. Come on in."

She nearly collapsed in relief as Finn ushered her through the door. She made a mental note to pinch Austin for scaring her.

His sandy hair was messy, void of his typically present ball cap, and he looked utterly at ease in a T-shirt, jeans and sneakers. He scooped a spoonful of ice cream from a bowl. "Welcome to your lovely home."

"Thanks," she answered, stepping aside so Finn could close the door.

"Ow!" Austin pressed a palm to his biceps. "You pinched me."

"You scared the daylights out of me."

Finn snorted behind her.

"And that's my ice cream," she continued, infinitely thankful to see Austin instead of a dangerous criminal. "Why didn't you call or text to let us know you were okay?" The rich, salty scent of warm grilled cheese reached her nose and she stiffened. "Are you cooking?"

Austin's wide smile returned. "Yeah. You should join us."

She followed his gaze to a narrow figure in the archway beyond. "Gage!"

The teen leaned against the jamb, long, narrow arms wrapped around his middle. His clothes and hair were dirty, and his cheeks were red with exposure from the sun. "I'm sorry—"

Hayley launched herself through the room, cutting off his unnecessary apology. "You're okay! I was so scared. I worried that you were hurt or abducted." *Or worse*, she thought, biting back the tears. She pulled him against her and rose onto tiptoes to tuck his head against her shoulder.

He hugged her back, instantly accepting the embrace. Then his thin body began to shake with stifled sobs.

"You're going to be okay now," she whispered. "I won't let anything bad happen to you. Neither will these guys. Or their family. Or the local police. And you're absolutely not going back to the Michaelsons."

He sucked in a ragged breath, regaining his composure and straightening with effort. He forced a tight smile through the tears. "I didn't mean to scare you."

"I was terrified," she said. "We think we know what you saw, and whoever is responsible for Kate's death might be following me too. Probably looking for you."

His eyes widened. "That's the reason I didn't come here

sooner. I was trying to make sure I didn't accidentally bring him here. I've been hiding and waiting until it was safe."

"I'm just glad you're here," she said, sliding her arm around his back and pulling him to her side. "How'd you get in?"

He frowned. "I came through your doggy door."

Austin moseyed in their direction, pulling an empty spoon from his mouth. "You really need to close that up or get a dog. Are you hungry?" He slid past them and headed for her stove.

The doggy door was tiny compared to the boy before her, but she supposed, if he managed to work his way inside, so could someone else. "Noted," she said. "And, yes. Something smells delicious."

Sounds of sizzling butter turned her to the stove, where Austin was loading another grilled cheese. "Good. We can talk over food."

Hayley searched the refrigerator for side dishes. "You are your mother."

Austin winked.

A few sliced apples and washed grapes later, the foursome settled around her small kitchen table. She nibbled on apples, too emotionally jarred to work up an appetite, but deeply satisfied with the turn of events.

Gage had come to her, just as she'd hoped. He trusted her to help him, which meant the world. More, Austin had been there to welcome and feed him. And the Beaumonts had prepared a place for him to stay safely on their ranch. Emotion stung her eyes and clogged her throat as she scanned the trio of men before her.

"Do you mind if I shower?" Gage asked. "I don't have anything else to wear, but I'd really like to wash up. Shampoo my hair. Maybe brush my teeth?"

Hayley nodded and stood, glad to be useful, when it seemed everyone else was doing things for her these days. "Of course. Come on. I have everything you need." She kept an assortment of travel-size toiletries for youths taken into emergency care without time to gather their things. Or others who simply didn't have anything of their own.

"I keep a change of clothes in my gym bag," Finn said. "You're welcome to wear that while I toss your outfit into the wash. It'll be a little big, but it's clean, and I'm guessing it'll fit better than anything in Hayley's closet."

Gage smiled, and the expression spread to the others.

The Beaumonts were broader, their bodies honed and matured, but Gage wasn't much shorter, and he'd likely be their height in the next year or two. He looked down the six-inch gap in height between himself and Hayley. "You're probably right about that."

Finn made a trip outside and returned with the bag.

Hayley walked Gage to the bathroom, then waited for him to toss his dirty clothes into the hallway.

"HE FIT THROUGH the doggy door?" Finn asked, eyeballing the small rubber flap across the room.

"Yep." Austin grinned. "You remember life at that age. He's a rack of growing bones. And I've got to be honest, I don't think he's eaten in a while."

Finn's jaw locked as he thought of Hayley feeding Gage and so many others lunch each workday. After meeting Mrs. Michaelson, he wasn't sure the kids in her care were getting much else, and he hoped the system moved quickly to review the family and extract the youths in their care.

"How was he otherwise?" Finn asked, knowing Austin would be a good judge. His brother had been around as many troubled teens as he had and would have insight.

There was a lot to infer from a kid's general disposition and unspoken vibe. Even Gage's mannerisms were likely to say more than the teen himself. Frequently, a combination of those things would reveal whether or not the individual might be willing to make healthy changes. Or if he was already determined to resist.

"I like him," Austin said, resting his backside against the sink and crossing his arms over his chest. "He was terrified when he saw me let myself inside, but once I mentioned Hayley's name and yours, he relaxed."

"Mine?" Finn worked the concept around his mind, unable to make sense of it. "How did he know my name?"

"Apparently the love of your life still talks about you too."

Finn frowned to stop his lips from smiling. He didn't have to ask how his brother had gotten inside. Austin was quite proud of his lock-picking skills. "Okay. What else?"

Austin held Finn's eye contact for a long beat before moving on. "He's polite, apologetic for his disappearance and the break-in. He stands tall, looks folks in the eyes and he washed his hands before eating. I'd say he was being raised right before whatever happened to his family."

"Car accident," Finn said. "Drunk driver on their weekly date night."

His brother's face paled, and he scrubbed a heavy hand over his hair. "That's horrible. He was where? Home with a sitter? Got a call from the hospital?"

Finn shook his head, feeling heat course through his chest. He'd looked into the case last night when he couldn't sleep, and what he'd found still haunted him. "The sitter fell through, and the kid begged them to go anyway. He was thirteen and convinced he could manage a couple of hours on his own while they had dinner. Mom reluctantly agreed. They ate at a restaurant two miles from home and died just outside their neighborhood. He heard the commotion but didn't think much of it until a sheriff came to the door. Apparently Mom's last words were about her son being home alone."

Austin's eyes shone with emotion, and he cussed.

"Yeah."

"What'd I miss?" Hayley asked, reappearing in the room like a ninja.

Austin spun away, and Finn cleared his throat. "We're just talking through our next steps."

"Good," she said. "We need a plan."

"I'll take his statement after he finishes in the shower," Finn said. "We'll have time while his clothes finish washing and drying. We can sit in the living room together. Someplace comfortable." He watched Hayley carefully, trying to determine her mood and mindset. "You should stick with him—he's clearly attached to you. He trusts you. We don't want him to hold back on anything or get scared."

She nodded, and her lips curled into a small prideful smile. "Agreed."

Austin pulled the dish towel from his shoulder and hung it over the sink's edge. "I'll tell him about the ranch and ask if he'd be willing to check it out. Then we can explain why it's the safest place for him right now and let him decide if he's willing to give it a chance. We don't want him running again."

"What if he says no?" Hayley asked, uncertainty in her eyes.

Finn lifted an arm toward the living room. Gage would likely finish showering soon, and finding all the adults holed up in the kitchen could give the wrong impression. They were definitely talking about him, but they weren't attempting to hide it from him. Better to get comfortable in the next room. In Finn's experience, transparency bred trust, and this kid needed to know they could all be trusted, not just Hayley. "Can we?"

She nodded, and they moved to the next room.

"If he doesn't like the ranch, he can stay at my place," Austin said, dropping onto the overstuffed armchair beside the couch. "It's cozy and well-protected. Food's not as good, but there are fewer kids and livestock to hassle him."

Finn rolled his eyes.

"And if you want him to stay someplace completely unconnected to the family," Austin added, "Scarlet can probably get us access to an empty home for a few nights. We can talk to the owners about paying rent for a few days."

Finn didn't hate that idea. Having a real-estate agent in the family had been surprisingly beneficial to the Beaumonts. "I like that."

The stairs creaked, and their heads turned collectively to see Gage.

His hair was mussed and damp. Finn's clothes hung from his narrow hips and shoulders, as expected, but something strange twisted in Finn's chest at the sight of him. He'd only met this kid an hour ago, but it was easy to understand why Hayley had become so attached. He was kind and vulnerable, but smart enough to make it on his own when he'd thought he was protecting Hayley. The intention alone was priceless.

"Come on down," Hayley said. "We were just talking about our next steps, and we need your input."

Gage's concerned expression morphed into surprise. He followed her request and settled on the couch between her and Finn. "What's up?"

Hayley told Gage about the ranch, and he listened, glancing to Austin and Finn a few times while she spoke.

"Is that where you want me to go?" he asked when she finished.

"I wish I could keep you with me, but I think the ranch is the best option for now," she said. "Until the killer is found, and you're safe again."

His skin paled at the word *killer*.

Finn accessed the recording feature on his phone. "I need to get an official statement from you about what you saw in Old Downtown the other night and anything before or after that you feel is relevant."

Gage took a deep breath and exhaled with a shudder. He rubbed his palms up and down his thighs, then wet his lips and nodded.

"Whenever you're ready," Finn said, pressing the button to begin the recording, then setting the device between them.

Gage set the stage, then spoke about his art, the thrumming bass of the nearby rave and the draw of people to the sound, like moths to the light. "I didn't see anyone go inside the other building, but I heard yelling in the pause between songs down the street. It sounded like a fight. Then the music came back, and I didn't hear the voices anymore, so I went across the street to see if I'd imagined them. I hadn't. There were two silhouettes inside the building marked for demolition. One was Kate. I'd talked to her earlier when a few of us were playing ball in the intersection. She'd explained how she was planning to fix up that part of Old Downtown, and she asked us what we thought was most important in a new shelter or community center. We all had things to say, and she listened. It seemed like she really wanted to get things right. She even said there would be part-time jobs for older teens to work with younger kids, packing lunches and getting them onto their buses for school when it starts again. At first it made sense to me that she'd be there, checking out the area, but it was kind of weird to see she was still there at night. And it was also hard to understand why anyone would argue with her. She was so kind. Still, I saw something move toward her, like a bat, maybe." His skin paled as he spoke. "Then she fell. A few seconds later, I heard a gunshot."

"Were you able to get a look at the person she was with?" Finn asked.

"No. They were behind the wall. I only had a glimpse at her through the broken window."

"Could you tell by the voice if it was a man or woman?" Finn asked.

Gage kneaded his hands together, brow furrowed in concentration. "Not for sure. I heard a woman's voice in that moment between the MC's voice and the next song, but I've been thinking about it, and I'm not sure if it was Kate's voice or not. It could've been a second woman, or it might've been her, and the other person could've been a man."

"Was she alone when she spoke to you earlier, when you were playing ball?" Finn asked.

"As far as I could see, yeah."

Hayley set a hand on his shoulder. "A man took a shot at me in that area, and a man stood outside the parking lot where I park for work."

Austin leaned forward. "Gage, when you ran, did you see who chased you?"

Finn considered the question. It was a good one. Typically, male criminals were more likely to give chase, and women tended to regroup and strategize, but there were exceptions to even the strongest rules. And he couldn't rely wholly on past scenarios to predict the future. Any murderer would have motivation to stop a witness before they reported what they'd seen.

Gage took another long beat to consider before he spoke. "I think it was a man. They seemed big, with heavy footfalls on the street. And they were close when I reached the rave. I thought I was caught, but the crowd was thick, and that building has a hole in the back wall. I ran to the opening, then ducked and doubled back instead of going out. I hid in the crowd until I thought it was safe to leave. I think whoever it was assumed I left."

Hayley swelled with pride. "That was smart. If they nearly caught you in a footrace to the rave, they might've gotten ahold of you if you'd tried your luck outside again."

He twisted on the cushion to look at her. "I was going to tell you everything the next day, but I kept thinking that maybe no one knew it was me. And maybe if I didn't say anything it would go away. Her body would be found, and the police would handle it. I didn't want to bring you into it or put myself in the spotlight."

She rubbed his back, and Finn's heart gave another heavy thud. Hayley was a natural at comforting hurting people. She had a heart for their pain, an internal drive to comfort. She'd make a perfect foster mom, and he was sure the court would give her a fair shot when this was over. From what he knows about the system between his connections and his family's, he was sure a judge would consider giving Hayley a chance at fostering Gage. The kid clearly accepted her as a mentor and confidante, and she would never let him down.

"Sorry I worried you," he whispered.

"Thank you for coming to me," Hayley responded.

Finn stopped the recording app and stood. They'd been at her home long enough for anyone watching to take notice. It was time to get moving, if they wanted to stay safe. "Who wants to see some livestock?"

Chapter Ten

Hayley leaned forward on her seat as Finn turned onto the long, familiar gravel lane. Returning to the Beaumont ranch for the first time in more than a year was nearly as breathtaking an experience as seeing it for the first time. She wished Gage had ridden with her so she could see his face as they arrived. Instead, he'd gone with Austin, who'd taken the lead in their little two-truck caravan.

She felt Finn's gaze on her cheek as her eyes widened in pleasure. Thick green grass rolled all the way to the horizon, split down the center by a dark ribbon of driveway and interspersed with fencing and livestock in their respective fields. The occasional human in a straw cowboy hat or colorful baseball cap waved an arm overhead as they rolled past.

Outbuildings, a large, impressive stable and several cabins dotted the land, each lovely, but none compared to the sprawling farmhouse before them. The Beaumont home spoke of generations of farmers and the decades of love bestowed upon it by this family.

Mr. and Mrs. Beaumont appeared on the porch as Finn parked his truck beside Austin's.

Hayley had to stop herself from running to greet them again. She hoped Gage would soon feel the same way. She wanted the family who meant so much to her to be important to him as well.

"Ready?" Finn asked, unfastening his seat belt.

"Always." She climbed down from the cab, taking a long beat to enjoy the view. Thick, dark mulch overflowed with bright blooms all around the farmhouse, and the arching cloudless blue sky stretched like a dome overhead.

Gage moved in her direction, nervous energy pouring off him in waves. The tension in his youthful face and posture set her slightly on edge.

"Give it a chance, okay?" She slid her arm beneath his and pulled him close, tipping her head back slightly to look up at his face. "I love this place and these people," she whispered, the words meant only for him. "They're not like anyone else I've ever known, and they're the very best of us. I'm sure of it."

His expression was grim, but he nodded. He was probably thinking of the last time Hayley had taken him to stay with a family. Look at how that had turned out. She needed to ask him more about the Michaelsons, and let him know what she thought of him not going back there for weeks, according to his foster mother, but this wasn't the right time. In this moment, she needed to give him the sense of peace and security he greatly deserved.

"Trust me," she urged, tugging his arm when he didn't look at her. She waited for those concerned brown eyes to fall on hers. Then she smiled. "If you aren't completely comfortable here before I leave, I will take you with me. That's a promise."

Gage pressed his lips together. "Austin said staying with you could put you in danger."

Hayley shook her head. "Staying at my house could put us in danger, but I'm not staying there right now, and I won't ask you to stay anywhere you aren't comfortable ever again."

He scrutinized her for a long moment before turning to the silent crowd on the Beaumonts' porch.

Finn and Austin had joined their parents, along with another brother, Lincoln, and the stable manager, Josi. All watched intently as she spoke to Gage.

"Look at them," she whispered again. "What's not to love?"

They all smiled brightly, eagerly, except Lincoln, who seemed to be sizing up Gage. He was probably already thinking of chores to keep the teen mentally engaged and physically exhausted. Josi looked at the brooding man beside her then elbowed his ribs.

Lincoln grunted and a partial smile bloomed on his face before he shut it down.

Hayley glanced at Finn, wondering if he'd caught the exchange, but his eyes were focused tightly on her. Fresh heat spread over her cheeks in response.

Gage straightened as if prepared for battle. "All right. I can do this. I don't want to put you in danger or cause you any more trouble."

"Hey." She stopped him as he tried to move forward. "You are not a burden to me. Understand? I'm only asking you to give them and this place a try. There's no wrong answer."

He nodded, not speaking.

"You are not a burden to me," she repeated, more slowly this time. "You are my friend, and I'm going to take care of you. These guys are going to help me. By the time I leave today, they'll all be your friends too. If they aren't, I meant what I said. Got it?"

"Yeah."

"Well?" Mrs. Beaumont asked from the bottom of the porch steps, nearly vibrating with excitement. "Will you stay?" she asked. "At least for the tour?"

"Sure," Gage agreed, and the older woman rushed to greet him.

"Can I hug you? I'm a hugger," she explained. "Isn't that right?"

The crowd murmured in confirmation, and Gage lifted his arms.

She wrapped him in a tight embrace, and within seconds, he hugged her back.

Hayley's eyes burned with appreciation. This was the safe place Gage needed, and she would be eternally grateful.

"It's lovely to meet you, Gage," Mrs. Beaumont said as she released him. "This is my family. You'll meet Dean soon, if you haven't already. I believe he's watching Hayley's place now. You know Finn and Austin. This is my husband, Garrett. I'm Mary. And this is Josi and Lincoln."

The family members took turns greeting him while Mrs. Beaumont fussed and Finn made his way to Hayley's side.

"I'm sure this isn't overwhelming at all," Finn teased, nudging her with his elbow.

She laughed, recalling the first time she'd been introduced to the family. The Beaumonts were wonderful, but they could be a lot. Especially upon introduction.

"Are you hungry?" Mrs. Beaumont asked, steering Gage up the porch steps toward the farmhouse door. "I always keep food and snacks on hand. Help yourself anytime. We have meals at…" The sound of her voice trailed off as the group followed inside.

"Do you remember the first time I brought you here?" Finn asked.

"How could I forget?" Hayley turned a bright smile on

him. "I thought you were all too good to be true. Gathering around that giant table for dinner, talking and laughing like friends. I was sure it was a show. I couldn't understand how you willingly spent so much time together and still liked one another."

Finn's eyebrows tented, then his expression slid into one of concern. "I sometimes forget my life isn't everyone else's normal. I wish it was."

"Me too."

He set a palm against her back and rubbed gently before pulling away.

Hayley felt the absence of his touch in her core, and maybe in her heart as well. She shook off the unwanted feeling and concentrated on the moment at hand. She needed to be sure Gage was at home on the ranch, then she needed to get back out there with Finn to see what they could learn about Kate's death. The sooner the killer was arrested, the sooner Gage wouldn't be in danger, and she could apply to be his guardian.

The farmhouse front door opened and Gage appeared, chatting with the young blond stable manager. Lincoln followed with his usual frown. All three members of the little group carried a bottle of water in one hand. The guys also held half of a sandwich.

"Not sure how Josi got away without being fed," Finn said. "Then again, she puts up with Lincoln all day every day, so we've suspected she was a magician for a while now."

Hayley laughed and raised her fingers in a wave as the trio passed.

Lincoln slowed. "We're giving the kid a tour."

Josi reached up to smack the brim of his hat. "His name is Gage."

Lincoln glared until she turned away, then grinned as he straightened his hat.

Finn shook his head, having clearly seen the exchange this time. "I don't get them."

Hayley fell into step behind the trio, giving them distance. Finn kept pace at her side.

"Do you have a dog?" Gage asked Lincoln.

"No."

"Really? Why not?" Gage frowned. "Don't they help with herding or something? You've got lots of room and the rescues are always full."

Lincoln looked past the teen to Josi, who grinned.

"He has a point," she said. "We've got miniature cows and donkeys, horses, goats and sheep. Chickens galore. No dog?"

Lincoln stopped suddenly and turned to pin Hayley with a curious stare. "Weren't you getting a dog last year?"

She'd wanted to badly but couldn't bring herself to take the plunge. "I decided I was gone too much to be the parent I wanted to be."

Josi looked to Gage. "Have you ever had a dog?"

The teen's cheeks paled and he nodded. "Larry."

"Where is he now?" Hayley asked, suddenly concerned he'd been forgotten in the chaos of losing Gage's parents. Had he been taken to the pound? Cast off somehow? Left to the streets?

"I got him when I was in preschool," Gage explained. "He died a few months before my parents. He was ten."

Josi's eyes shone with emotion and darted to Lincoln.

"Ten's a good long life for a dog," Lincoln said. "We've had a few over the years that only made it to eight or nine, but they were loved. They were happy."

Gage nodded. "Yeah."

Hayley's stomach tightened with the new knowledge. She'd had no idea he'd lost a lifelong friend and his parents in the same year. "I'm going to get a dog soon," she blurted, drawing the eyes of all three companions.

"Really?" Gage asked, his expression both stunned and hopeful.

"Mmm-hmm," she said, processing the possibility at warp speed. "I plan to work less overtime soon, so I'll be home for dinner every night, and the office is near enough for me to walk him at lunchtime." She could set up her cooler at the usual picnic table before she left. Maybe even bring the dog on some work-related visits.

"Let's go," Lincoln said, clapping Gage on the shoulder. "We'll check out the stable and your cabin while they talk." He lifted his chin to indicate something behind Hayley.

She turned to find Austin making his way across the field.

"Are you running from me?" he called as Lincoln led Gage and Josi through the open barn doors.

"Always," Lincoln hollered, then vanished inside.

Finn set his hands on his hips and turned to his approaching brother. "Any news?"

"Nope. One of my informants says he was at the rave that night. Saw a kid fitting Gage's description tear through the place. That was all he remembered. Most folks were high, so everyone he asked today had no idea what he was talking about."

Hayley groaned. "So there aren't any new leads on who was chasing him."

Or who'd killed Kate.

"So what's next?" she asked.

Finn rolled his shoulders and squinted against the sun. "I'll check in with the officers who stayed in Old Downtown to do interviews. Maybe something someone said will be a clue, even if it isn't a definitive ID of the killer."

Austin rubbed his palms. "I'll head back to the office and dig into Kate's social-media accounts. I'll look at everyone on her friends lists, check out her posts, read their posts, see who she interacted with on the days leading up to her death. The usual."

Familiar laughter turned Hayley back to the barn, where Gage was leading the pack in her direction.

"I like it here," he called. "You were right. I want to stay."

A long breath of relief rushed from her chest. "If that's what you want."

"I do." He smiled widely as he reached her, then wrapped her in a hug. "Thank you."

Lincoln's lips twitched, and Hayley felt her eyebrows raise. The fleeting expression looked a lot like a smile. Three in an hour had to be a new record for him. "In that case," he said, pulling a cell phone from his pocket, "this is for you. We set it up when we heard you were coming. It's got all our numbers in there and Hayley's."

"Seriously?" Gage asked, obviously flabbergasted.

"Yep."

Gage accepted the phone with an expression of pure joy. "This is sick!"

Hayley tamped down the rush of emotion, laughing outwardly at the roller coaster of feelings she'd been on today. "You can call me if you need anything. Even if you're just bored or lonely."

"Or if Lincoln gets on your nerves," Josi offered.

The group laughed, but Lincoln pinned her with his grumpiest of looks.

"I'll be his favorite in a day or two," Lincoln said. "Now

let's check out your mini apartment." He turned and headed for the small cabins behind the stable.

Gage shot Hayley a stunned look. "Apartment?"

"Everyone staying on-site has their own space," she explained as they all followed Lincoln. "Those larger cabins belong to Lincoln and Josi. The smaller ones are used for teens staying here on a short-term basis."

"This one," Lincoln said, stopping at the door to a unit near his own, "is for you."

Finn crossed his arms and leaned toward Hayley as his brother unlocked the door. "This one is usually used for storage, so it's a work in progress."

"Ranch was full," Austin added, inserting himself into the exchange. "But there wasn't any stopping Mama when she heard about your situation."

Hayley watched as the group filed inside.

"Are you serious?" Gage's voice carried through the open door to her heart. "Hayley! You've got to see this!"

She darted forward, slipping into the former storage unit before coming to an immediate halt. The Beaumonts had arranged a twin bed and small desk on one wall. A chest of drawers on another. The bed was covered in a navy blue blanket and topped with a puffy white pillow. An oval throw rug covered the floor. The desk doubled as a nightstand with a lamp positioned closest to the headboard. An open notebook contained a two-word message in bright blue letters.

Welcome, Gage!

Hayley looked first at Josi, then at each Beaumont with silent adoration. "Thank you."

Gage dragged his eyes from the notebook to Hayley. "This is where I get to stay while I'm here? In this cabin?"

"Yep," Austin answered, then reached beneath the desk to open the door to a pint-size refrigerator. "We stocked this with drinks and snacks. Kids your age keep ridiculous hours, and we thought you'd rather have some things at your place than go hungry or make the trek to our folks' house at two a.m."

"My place," Gage repeated, awestruck.

Finn shifted, reminding Hayley he was still right there at her side. "Only until we find the person who killed Kate and chased you. I don't plan to let that take long."

Gage's smile filled the room. "How old do you have to be to stay here?"

"At the ranch?" Josi asked.

He nodded. "Hayley said the other kids will be removed from the Michaelsons' home. I looked after them when I could, especially Parker. He's eight."

"You're probably the youngest," Josi said. "We typically host kids closer to high-school graduation. Some are even my age on occasion."

"We look at each applicant on a case-by-case basis," Lincoln said. "Eight is too young to be here, I think. Not everyone we host is in a good place emotionally. You're in danger, and you've been through a lot, but you seem like you've got a clear head. Not all our kids do."

Gage's expression fell, and his brow creased in concern. "Where will Parker go?"

"Someplace nice and safe," Hayley promised. "I'll personally interview each family to be sure they're up to par this time."

"When will he move?" he asked.

"Soon. I've requested a review of the home and one-on-

one interviews for the kids. Without the Michaelsons listening or influencing them in any way. The children will have the freedom to speak candidly."

Something in Gage's expression said he didn't think that was good enough, but Hayley didn't press the issue. She told herself to take his willingness to stay with the Beaumonts as a win and she'd let the social workers handling the Michaelsons do their jobs. She had a good team at the office and in front of her.

Finn's phone buzzed and he removed it from his pocket to look at the screen. "If you're set here, we should take off," he said, looking to Gage, then Hayley.

The sudden tension in his jawline set her feet in motion. She gave each of the individuals before her a hug, adding an extra squeeze to Gage before stepping back. "Call me if you need anything, and I'll be here in under thirty minutes."

"I'm good," he assured.

"If anything changes," she said, backing through the door and into the grass.

"Take care of him," she called, turning to follow Finn, who was already moving toward his truck.

He stopped to catch her hand and urge her into a jog.

"What happened?" she asked, on high alert as they launched into his cab and peeled out of the driveway.

Finn placed his portable emergency light on the roof and hit the gas "There was a break-in at your office."

Chapter Eleven

Finn piloted his truck into the lot outside the social-services office. A pair of Marshal's Bluff cruisers were already in place. A uniformed officer stood guard at the door. The building had closed for the day only a short while earlier, so whoever had broken in hadn't waited long to act.

Typically, break-ins were executed under cover of night and at a location with items of high resale potential. Whatever the criminal had been seeking was likely only valuable to one person, and Finn suspected that person was searching for Gage Myers. The timing, when factored in with Kate's murder and the witness who'd gotten away, was too coincidental. And Finn didn't believe in coincidences.

"I can't believe this is happening," Hayley whispered, releasing her safety belt as he pulled his key from the ignition.

He climbed out and met her on the sidewalk. "How do you feel about working the scene together?"

She raised her eyebrows. "You want my help in there?"

As a general rule, he did his best to keep civilians away from crime scenes, but Hayley was familiar with the case and location in ways no one else on-site was, making her invaluable. Not to mention, he preferred to keep her close. For her safety and his sanity. "I'll do the talking and interacting with staff and officers," he said. "You evaluate the office. This is your territory. You'll know better than anyone if something is missing or has been left behind. Take your time and concentrate. If there's a mess, it could be a distraction. If something new has appeared, I need to know that too. The item could be a camera or recording device. Make note of anything that feels off."

Her expression morphed from shock to resolve, and she nodded. "Got it."

Finn held her gaze one moment longer, then took the lead as they approached the officer at the door.

"Detective Beaumont," the older gentleman said, accepting Finn's outstretched hand for a quick shake.

Finn stepped aside, allowing Hayley to pass. "This is—"

"Hi, Don," she said sweetly, pausing inside the small vestibule. "How's Cora?"

"Better every day," the older officer said. "I'll let her know you asked about her."

"Thank you."

Finn matched Hayley's pace as they moved through the quiet hallway. "How do you know Don?"

"Through his wife. She had a pretty serious surgery last month. I brought dinner once or twice. They're good people. Do you know them well?"

"Barely at all." Even in a department as small as his, everyone had a job to do, and it was easy to stay busy. He rarely spent any real time with anyone outside his immediate team.

A pair of men in suits appeared at the open door to Social Services. They bent their heads together as they moved away, each carrying a stack of files and loose papers.

"They work in human resources," Hayley whispered, then waved. "Caleb, Frank."

The men stopped, looking curiously at their coworker.

Finn extended a hand to each man in turn. "Hello, I'm Detective Beaumont."

They both murmured quick hellos.

"What can you tell us about the break-in?" Finn asked.

Their collective attention swung back to Hayley, as they were probably wondering why she was there and was being accompanied by a detective.

The taller of the pair was first to respond. He cleared his throat and forced a tight smile in Finn's direction. "I'm Caleb Morrison, the management leader here. I organize and facilitate the teams. I also act as a liaison between all staff and administration." His gaze slid briefly to Hayley before returning to Finn. "The break-in appears to have been directed at Ms. Campbell or someone on her caseload. Beyond that, I'm not sure."

The heavier man at Caleb's side wiggled his blue-gloved fingers. "I'm Frank Riggs. These files were tossed out of the cabinets in our portion of the offices. We're supposed to see if anything's missing. We barely print anything these days, so unless someone was searching for something from years ago, all this mess was likely for show. Or the result of a hissy fit."

Hayley snorted lightly, then covered her nose with one hand. "Sorry."

Finn fought a smile.

"Someone is hot for one of your cases," Frank said, looking much more serious. "I'd stick with this guy as much as you can until this is sorted." He tipped his head at Finn and scanned him appreciatively. "Shouldn't be a hardship."

Hayley took Finn's elbow in her hand and tugged him away, waving goodbye to Frank and Caleb with her free hand.

"I like Frank," Finn said.

Hayley laughed, and the sound warmed his heart.

A second officer stood guard inside the social-services door and raised his chin in greeting.

Before Finn could ask the man for information, Hayley gasped. He followed her wide-eyed stare to a crime-scene photographer, snapping shots of an absolute disaster. Presumably Hayley's desk.

The rolling chair had been overturned on its mat. All the metal drawers were open. Trinkets, framed photos, toys and keepsakes littered the floor and desktop. Office supplies were fanned across the carpet.

It seemed Frank had been on the right track. This certainly looked like the site of a recent hissy fit. Not at all what Finn had anticipated.

The photographer stepped away, and Finn donned a pair of gloves, then passed a second set to Hayley. "I guess it's time to get to work. Tell me about the space."

The room was large and divided into sections by groups of desks, presumably the teams Caleb had mentioned.

Hayley tugged the gloves over her trembling hands. "This is my desk. These belong to my team members." She swung a pointed finger from desk to desk. "Those are the other teams, and that door leads to Human Resources and Administration." Her voice cracked, and she released a thin, shaky breath.

"You okay?"

"I can do this," she assured him quietly, then crouched to examine the mess.

Finn scanned the bigger picture first, then slowly pulled his attention inward to the single destroyed workstation.

Everything else appeared untouched and utterly ignored.

The office was in need of sprucing up. The carpet was threadbare, while the wall paint was chipping and faded.

"Recognize these desks?" she asked, rising to her feet once more. "They were handed down to us from the police station after your renovations last year."

Finn grimaced. He hadn't recognized them, but he'd certainly noticed they were old.

"They're a step up from what we had," she said, probably reading his expression. "We were glad to get them, and it's nice they didn't go straight to a landfill somewhere. Our desks went to other places in need. A church office and some homeschooling moms, I believe."

Finn made a mental note to circle back to the topic of funding for Social Services when he had more time. His family would surely have ideas on how to help the department who helped everyone else.

"What do you think?" she asked.

"I think someone knew what they were after and where to find it."

"The guy who's been following me," she mused.

Finn nodded, then raised his hand to a passing crime-scene technician. "Are you finished here?"

The young man gave the room a glance. "We're wrapping up now. We've got all we need."

"Anything you can share that might help me?"

"Afraid not," the man said. "No prints. No signs of a break-in. The alarm was triggered at the interior point of entry." He pointed to a keypad on the wall inside the social-services area.

Finn considered that a moment. "Someone accessed the building before closing and waited until the coast was clear to make his way in here."

"That's my guess," the tech said. "I'll get the photos over to you along with lab analysis on a couple small things. Hair. Mud. Probably left by workers or clients, but both were in the line of fire, so I'm taking a closer look." He tipped his head to the overturned chair.

"Appreciate it," Finn said.

"Can I clean up, Ryan?" Hayley asked.

"Okay by me," the tech said. "But Beaumont's the boss."

"Well, don't tell him that too often," she teased. "We'll all pay the price."

Hayley collected an armload of her things from the floor as the tech took his leave. "Ryan and I met a few months ago. His wife teaches second grade, and I had one of her students on my caseload. She introduced us."

Finn shook his head. Everyone who met Hayley was instantly charmed. Not because she was perfect, but because she was honest and real.

She narrowed her eyes, but before she could voice her thoughts, Caleb appeared with a frown.

"Detective?" he asked.

Finn snapped easily back to work mode. "Find something?"

"No. We've been through all the folders. Everything appears to be in order."

"Thank you." Finn set his hands on his hips and looked at the open door to Human Resources. What had made the burglar dig through the paper files? "You took your laptop home with you?" he asked Hayley.

"Yes. Why?"

It was possible that whoever had come for her computer might've tried the filing cabinets as the next most logical place to find information on a case.

"Just theorizing," he said. "The interior alarm was already triggered when they came in, so they had to hurry, then leave empty-handed. Explains the hissy fit."

She grinned.

Finn went to wrap things up with the officers on duty while Hayley rearranged and tidied her desk.

An image of her in his arms at a fundraiser caught his eye upon return. A dozen bright, youthful faces filled the space at their sides. They'd made huge differences for the betterment of their community when they were together. He'd thought they'd grow old doing those same things.

What had gone so wrong? And how had he not seen it coming?

HAYLEY PACKED A few more of her things during a quick trip home, then rejoined Finn in his truck. "Thanks," she said, buckling up for the ride back to his place.

It hadn't occurred to her, until the break-in at her office, that there were a number of little things she'd like to protect in case there was a burglary. She would've been safe at Finn's place, but her precious photos, mementos and keepsakes were irreplaceable too. So she'd been thrilled when he hadn't objected to her picking up a little more of her stuff.

"Any chance you have a spare key on you?" he asked, dropping his cell phone into the truck's cupholder. "And would you mind if Dean or Austin replace your locks with a keypad version as soon as possible? Something we'll be able to monitor? Maybe one of those doorbells with a camera too."

"They can have mine," she said, lifting a key between them. "Whatever makes my home safer is perfect." Especially since she hoped to share the place with Gage when this was over.

Finn took the key and shifted into Drive.

It broke her heart to think of how close she'd come to spending her life with him, and how she'd ruined it by waiting far too long to face her demons.

Soon the familiar home appeared, situated atop a hill with mature trees and plenty of lush green grass. Enough room for chubby toddler legs to run and growing childhood bodies to play. The wide gravel swath outside an attached garage had ample space for guests, family and friends to park. Even enough for future teenage drivers she'd once believed would belong to her and Finn.

Never underestimate how much can change in a year, she thought.

Or the limits on how badly one person can mess up.

A few moments later, Finn unlocked the front door and waited for her in the kitchen while she delivered her things to the guest room. She returned to him with squared shoulders. Things between them couldn't go back to the way they were, but they could certainly be improved. And that started with an explanation for her behavior last year. Finn would never bring up something so painfully personal in the midst of a serious investigation. She, on the other hand, needed to say her piece. She owed him at least that much.

Finn clapped his hands as she emerged from the hallway. "Austin's on his way over to grab that house key, and I've made some sandwiches. Nothing fancy, but I'm hungry and thought you might be too. Also, I'm hoping we can brainstorm."

Haylcy froze. The sudden change of mental direction nearly gave her whiplash.

He passed her a plate with a handful of kettle chips and a pickle spear beside a sandwich cut into two triangles.

"BLT," he said. "I microwaved the leftover bacon from breakfast."

She took a seat at the island, unsure she could eat until she got a few secrets off her chest. Her attention caught on a large whiteboard with wheels in the living area.

"For the brainstorming," he said around a mouthful of sandwich.

She blinked. "Right."

Finn wiped his mouth, looking ten years younger at home than he did on the job. He'd turned a baseball hat around on his head and visibly relaxed down to his toes. It was easy to remember he was twenty-five when he was on duty. At home, like this, it was hard to believe he wasn't late for class somewhere. "Now that Gage is safe, we can redirect our attention. Uniformed officers have done preliminary interviews with Kate's family and staff. I'll go over the official transcripts before we start knocking on doors."

He rose and crossed the room to grab his satchel and a laptop. He set the latter beside her plate, then freed a second laptop from his bag. "Are you still a magician when it comes to social-media stalking?"

Hayley reluctantly set aside her need for confession and willed herself to refocus. Finn wanted her help now. The rest could wait.

"Hayley?" he coaxed. "You okay?"

She refreshed her smile. "I believe stalking is illegal, Detective, but I'm still quite good at research."

"Excellent." Finn opened the lid on his laptop. "I was hoping you'd say that. I'm looking for details on all the latest posts and interactions from Kate. Austin usually helps with this, but he's spread thin. If you find something you want him to dig into, he can. Otherwise, let's see how much progress we can make tonight. I'll read all the interviews and anything else that's been added to the case file while you search, and we'll see what stands out."

"Deal." She raised her half sandwich to him in a toast.

Several hours later, her eyes stung, and her body ached from being hunched over the laptop. She stood and stretched.

"Anything?" he asked.

"Nothing's screaming *motive* to me," she admitted, "but I generally see the good in people so—"

He set aside his laptop and turned to face her. "What are your overall thoughts and insights?"

She considered his question and what she'd learned that could be relevant. "I hadn't realized Kate's husband had such a Cinderella story. His family was practically homeless when he met her. The fact his path ever crossed hers is a miracle. For them to fall in love, get married and make it eight years together is probably like winning the lottery. Literally and figuratively." Hayley wasn't sure how she felt about it. Happy for the couple, but also a little suspicious, because money was the number-one reason for divorce—she felt somewhat guilty for thinking the last part.

Finn rolled his shoulders and arched his back, apparently as stiff and uncomfortable as she'd been. "Paul was poor before they married?"

"Very much. He was working at a YMCA when she came to see how she could help. Then poof. Love."

Finn grunted. "I'll see if there's a prenup. If so, I'll need to know what he stood to lose if the marriage fell apart."

Hayley frowned. "Am I a sappy dope if I really don't want that to pan out? Not another man who vowed to love, honor and cherish his wife only to murder her for her money."

"No." The smile on Finn's face was brittle, and she flinched when her phone buzzed.

"It's my coworker," she said, lifting the device to read the message. "The kids are being removed from the Michaelsons' home tomorrow morning."

Finn's expression brightened a moment before he went into work mode. "That's good."

"Yeah," she said, feeling the first flutters of nerves return. "Finn?"

"Yeah?"

Hayley inhaled deeply, then spoke the words that had been on her heart for a year. "I'm sorry I ran away when you proposed."

He tensed and the air thickened…and all evidence of the carefree young man disappeared.

"It wasn't because I didn't love you, or because I didn't want to marry you, because I did. More than anything." She paused to let him process, then searched for the strength to go on.

His jaw tensed and flexed, but his body was otherwise motionless.

"I've told you my mom drinks," Hayley went on. "That she's unreliable, difficult and mean. I didn't tell you how bad it was growing up with her. It was awful." Hayley nearly choked on the words. Nothing she could say would make it better or believable. If she hadn't lived her life, seen it with her eyes, experienced it herself, she'd never have believed a mother could be like hers. The way she probably still was. "She was supposed to love and protect me. She did not. And she stood by while the men in her life hurt me too." Tears sprung to her eyes, and her chin jutted forward in defiance to everyone who'd tried to make her a terrible, hateful human. "I hadn't dealt with that pain or processed the trauma, and in a very twisted way, your profession of love and desire to protect me felt like betrayal. It triggered all these suppressed, ignored, bottled-up feelings and I just…ran."

The same way she'd run away from her mother's trailer. The way she'd run from almost everything good in her life before it could hurt her too. Only her job had ever given her joy without fear, and that was probably because she worked hard and faced her share of troubles, according to her therapist. She trusted that joy, because she'd felt she'd earned it. "I know now that I don't have to earn love and that I am deserving of it as well. But I didn't know that then."

Finn's Adam's apple bobbed. "You don't owe me an explanation."

"You're right. I owe you a whole lot more. You didn't deserve the pain I caused you. I want you to know I'm getting the help I need, and I'm doing better all the time. I shouldn't have waited so long to get myself together." She locked her eyes on Finn, desperate for him to understand what she couldn't say. She'd do anything to take back the moment she'd ran. Because she knew now, from a healed perspective, he'd have stayed with her through it all. "I didn't believe something as wonderful as you could be meant for someone as damaged as me."

Regret swelled her tongue and halted her words. Then the tears began to fall.

Finn stepped carefully forward and opened his arms as an offering.

Part of her longed to turn and leave.

Instead, she stepped into his embrace and let him cradle her protectively against his chest until the tears ran dry.

Chapter Twelve

The muffled sound of a ringing phone drew Hayley from a restless sleep. She groaned with the crash of memories. She'd confessed her soul to Finn, then she'd cried herself to sleep. He'd barely said a word.

The past few days' worth of tension and fear had poured out of her, along with a lifetime of heartache and pain. She'd only intended to tell Finn as much as necessary to clear the air, but instead a dam had burst. She wasn't able to stop her words or tears until she'd become completely deflated.

Like the man he was, Finn had held her, comforted her, then walked her to bed so she could rest and recover. Despite the fact she'd hurt him. Despite the fact she'd unleashed a torrent of emotion without warning. Despite the fact she'd basically ambushed him. He'd even brought her a cold, wet cloth for her eyes. A glass of water and a couple of Tylenol to prevent a headache.

Hayley rolled onto her side and pulled the pillow over her head in residual horror. Finn hadn't been angry that she'd kept so much of herself from him while they were together. He didn't tell her that none of it mattered now, because they were over. He'd just been there. Strong and silent. Giving her the emotional space to fall apart while he held her together.

Then he'd left her alone with her demons.

At least she wouldn't have to face him for a few more hours. The first rays of sunlight were barely visible on the horizon beyond her window. With a little luck, she'd be ready to face him by the time the day began.

Her ears pricked when the muffled voice in the next room said Gage's name. Instinct made her sit upright and tightened her nerves. She stared at her closed bedroom door, hyperfocused on each low warble as the words came faster, desperate to dissect the meanings.

"I'm waking her now," Finn said suddenly, right outside her room.

Panic pushed her onto her feet. "Come in."

The door opened, and Finn's eyes met hers with alarm.

"What happened?" she asked, fear swirling in her anxious heart and muddled mind.

"Gage is missing."

THIRTY MINUTES LATER, Hayley burst from Finn's pickup and onto the grass outside his family's farmhouse.

Mrs. Beaumont waited on the wide wraparound porch. "Come in. I made breakfast and put on the coffee." She opened her arms to embrace them, then ushered them inside.

Hayley's lip trembled at the warm reception. She was thankful for the love of a mother when she needed it most, even if the mother wasn't hers. "Thank you."

The oversize eat-in kitchen smelled of biscuits and gravy. Beaumont men sat at the nearby table and hovered around an island the size of a boat. Josi filled mugs with coffee at the counter.

The family quieted as they took note of Hayley's arrival.

She stroked flyaway hairs away from her puffy eyes and swollen cheeks. The haphazard ponytail she'd wrangled into place on the drive between homes was already falling over one shoulder. She could only imagine what she looked like. She hadn't been brave enough to meet her own eyes in the bathroom mirror while brushing her teeth and hair.

Josi passed her a steaming mug. "I'm so sorry."

Lincoln stepped forward, into the space behind the young blonde, before Hayley could form words. "We don't know what happened," he said, jaw tense and eyes hard. "Gage was happy when we left him to settle in for bed. This morning, he was gone. He took his phone, but he won't answer."

"Why would he do that?" Hayley whispered, posing the question to herself as much as to the others.

"That's what I keep saying," Lincoln grumbled. "Doesn't make any sense."

Josi passed Finn a mug when he joined them at the counter.

The warmth of his nearness added a small measure of comfort to Hayley's weary soul.

"Have you thoroughly checked his room?" Finn asked. "Notice signs of trouble? Maybe a note?"

The responding death glare from Lincoln raised the fine hairs on Hayley's neck. "Of course, I have," he said.

Josi shifted discreetly, angling her body by an inch until her shoulder brushed Lincoln's chest.

His gaze flickered to her before jerking back to his brother. "I'm well aware of what to look for when a kid goes missing," he added, only slightly less hostile. "This isn't my first rodeo, and you know it."

Finn raised a palm. "I'm just trying to ask what you found."

"Nothing. That's the problem," Lincoln stormed. "The place is spotless. Nothing's missing except him and his phone."

Hayley thought about Finn's advice to her at the office crime scene. "Did Gage happen to leave anything behind? Something you didn't provide?" Something to suggest he planned to come back?

"Yeah. These," Josi said, pulling a folded row of photo-booth pictures from her back pocket. "I brought them along to help the search party."

Hayley took the strip gingerly. "There's a search party?"

Josi nodded. "They went out about twenty minutes ago. Lincoln went over to wake him around five thirty on his way to the stables. He looked around for a few minutes, thinking he'd just gone out to walk or clear his head. As soon as we realized he was nowhere near, I reached out to some of the farm hands just starting their days, then headed over here to let the Beaumonts know. Lincoln called Finn, and the others fanned across the property. No word so far."

Finn leaned closer, peering at the strip of black-and-white images in her hand. "That's Parker."

Hayley nodded. The pair were closer than she'd realized.

"Who?" Lincoln asked.

"Another boy staying with the same foster family," Finn explained. "He said Gage took care of him whenever he was there."

Fresh alarm shot through Hayley as she dragged her gaze from the photos to Finn. "All the kids are being removed from the Michaelsons' care today. Including Parker."

Josi sucked in a small, audible breath. "He's the boy Gage asked about. He wanted to know how old kids had to be to stay here."

Hayley felt herself begin to nod, recalling Gage's question. In all the chaos, she'd completely forgotten.

Josi had told him Parker was too young.

FINN MARCHED ONTO the Michaelsons' porch at just after eight. He knocked more forcefully than necessary, then waited impatiently with Hayley at his side.

She'd spoken by phone with the social worker who'd reviewed the Michaelsons at her request. The other woman had found the couple lacking and confirmed the children would only be there another few hours. She was on her way to begin the process now.

Finn knocked again.

The front door sucked open with force, and Mrs. Michaelson glared out. A cacophony of voices and noise filled the home behind her. "Ugh," she groaned. "You again. Haven't you done enough? Sending people out here to ask a bunch of questions, disrupt the kids' days and poke through my life. Go away."

"Mrs. Michaelson," Finn began calmly, raising a palm to indicate she would be wise to wait. "We're here to speak with Parker." With a little luck, the kid had spoken to Gage last night. If Gage had used his new phone to call the Michaelsons' residence, Parker might even know where to find the older boy.

The sound of approaching vehicles drew his attention over one shoulder. A cruiser and unmarked sedan pulled into the space behind his truck at the curb.

The sedan was expected, but a uniformed officer was not.

"Why are the police here?" Hayley asked, gaze jumping to Finn.

"Haven't you heard?" Mrs. Michaelson asked. "Parker's gone."

"What do you mean he's gone?" Hayley cried.

A woman in tan pants and a navy blouse jogged up the steps to join them. She frowned at Hayley. "I just got the call. I changed directions and came right over as soon as I heard. I haven't even been to the office."

"I don't understand," Hayley said, eyes pleading. "Are you saying Parker ran away too?"

The uniformed officers were next to reach the porch. Officer Young tipped his head in greeting. "Mrs. Michaelson called to report a missing child this morning. We're here to take the report and interview the family."

Finn pointed to the nearby trash bin, filled to the brim with beer cans and empty alcohol containers. "You'll want to make note of that. The contents have doubled since the last time I was here."

"Hey now," Mrs. Michaelson protested, opening the door to allow the officers to pass. "Why don't you mind your business," she suggested. "Maybe concentrate on finding Gage, because he's still not here."

Finn held the door when the woman stepped out of the officers' way. He waved for Hayley and her coworker to enter ahead of him, then paused to level Mrs. Michaelson with an icy look. "If you're exposing vulnerable children to parties serving that much alcohol, or worse, you and your husband are putting it away on your own, that is absolutely our business."

Three middle schoolers at the kitchen counter went silent.

"Where's Mr. Michaelson now?" Officer Young asked. "We're hoping to catch him before he leaves for work."

"Already gone," Mrs. Michaelson reported, shoving the door shut behind the crowd. "He's a fisherman. Boat leaves before dawn, and he's always on it."

Hayley and her coworker went into business mode, instructing the children to gather their things.

The officers walked Mrs. Michaelson to the kitchen table to take her statement.

Finn took a spin around the first floor, looking for additional signs of trouble. The rooms were relatively tidy, considering the number of kids under the roof. According to the coat hooks and cubbies on the kitchen wall, there were five children in total at the modest suburban home. Pieces of masking tape with neat black letters spelled the names Gage, Parker, Orion, Wesley and Trent. Hopefully, one of the latter would be cooperative and helpful in finding Gage and Parker.

He paused in the kitchen to listen while Mrs. Michaelson relayed her timeline of events, beginning last night and ending this morning. "Ms. Campbell and I spoke with Parker when we were here before," he said, interrupting. "He said Gage goes home when he takes off. Any idea what that means?"

The officers raised their eyebrows in interest.

Mrs. Michaelson crossed her arms. "No. This is his home. Or it was."

Officer Young pursed his lips, presumably in thought. "Whatever happened to his family's place?"

"I assume it sold," Finn said. "It's been a while."

Hayley reappeared with one of the boys, a pillow and his bag. "I can check the county auditor's site."

"I've got this," Finn said. Dean's fiancé was a Realtor. If they needed any additional information on the home or property, he'd give his brother a call. Hayley had her hands full with more important things.

"Okay." She led the boys and her coworker outside to help settle them in the sedan.

"Where are they going?" Mrs. Michaelson complained.

Finn left the officers to handle the angry woman, then joined Hayley in his truck.

She looked exhausted and disheveled as she climbed aboard once more. "Any chance we can trace the cell phone Lincoln gave Gage?" she asked. "Get a list of numbers he called or everyone who called the Michaelsons' landline since last night? Confirm whether or not Gage contacted Parker?"

"You're certain they're together?" Finn asked, feeling the truth of the words as he spoke. The boys' united disappearance was another coincidence too big to ignore.

She nodded. "I'm sure of it."

"Josi told Gage that Parker was too young for the ranch," Finn said, shifting into Drive and thinking aloud. "Gage thought Parker wasn't safe with the Michaelsons, and this is Gage's way of protecting him?"

"I think so," Hayley said. "Which is hard to get my head around considering the danger Gage is in. How can he possibly protect a little kid and himself while on the run? Parker would've been safe and happy if Gage would've given us time to place him in another home."

"But Gage is new to the system," Finn said, suddenly more tired than he'd been in a very long time. "You and I know the Michaelsons are the exception to the rule, and that wherever Parker is placed next will likely be filled with love and compassion. But this was Gage's only experience in foster care. He has no idea how good things can be, only how bad they've been."

Hayley raised her cell phone. "I'm going to try Gage's number again." She turned away and left a pleading voice mail, begging him to return to the ranch. She assured him it was okay to take Parker with him, and she vowed to protect them both.

Finn focused on the road, willing the rest of their day to get significantly better than the start.

Chapter Thirteen

Hayley concentrated on her breaths as Finn drove along the bay toward Old Downtown. It seemed like the most reasonable place to start their search for Gage and Parker. Gage was known to spend time in the area, and there were plenty of places for two boys to hole up and hide out. She hated the thought of them being there, especially knowing how many things could go wrong, but she also hoped they were somewhere in those neglected blocks, so she and Finn could find them and bring them home.

Sunlight twinkled off cresting waves and brilliant blue water, creating a postcard-worthy view beyond her window. Warm southern sun heated her skin, the familiar humidity cocooning her through the open window as they slowed for a turn.

Hayley kneaded her hands.

"We'll start on the outskirts," Finn said. "Talk to everyone we see, just like we did that first day. Then we'll move inward, toward the heart of the area, and finally toward the waterfront properties where the rave was held and Kate's body was located."

Hayley crossed and uncrossed her legs, knee bobbing as they rolled toward their destination. "I'm glad it's still early. I'm willing to turn over every piece of trash and rubble down here if needed." And thanks to the long summer days, she'd have nearly twelve more hours of light to do it.

"I don't think it'll come to that," Finn said. "Gage is trying to protect Parker, so he'll be strategic about where he takes him."

She stared into the distance, where traffic vanished along with all signs of grass and trees, replaced with sprawling concrete and desolation, dark storefronts with painted windows and barred doors. "That's what bothers me about him coming here. Gage knows what safe means. He had it with his family. If he's here now, I don't think he plans to stay longer than necessary. Which makes finding them fast even more important."

Finn glanced Hayley's way, his eyes skimming her face, then his gaze dropped to her twisting hands and bouncing knee. "I got the feeling most people in Old Downtown knew Gage, or at least recognized him from his art. He's spent a lot of time down here. His shadow children are everywhere. Chances are he talked to someone long enough to make friends. Maybe he went to them for help with Parker. Maybe he shared something that will lead us to the place he's calling home."

Hayley inhaled deeply and shook her hands out at the wrists. "You're right. I need to stay positive and focused." No more letting her unbearably negative imagination run away.

The truck slowed along the curb near a highway overpass, and Finn's attention moved to his rearview mirror.

"What is it?" Hayley turned, noticing a black SUV behind them.

The other vehicle sat on the previous block, angled against the curb as if it had pulled over as suddenly as they had. The SUV stood out as badly as Finn's truck in this area. It was shiny and new, while the rides parked between them were old and rusted.

"That SUV's been following us," Finn said. "It's not the same make or model as the one from the news, but it's been back there since we turned off Bay View. If we're being tailed because they're also looking for the boys, I need to know. And if we're being tailed for some other reason, I should probably know that too."

Her stomach churned as he opened his door. "Where are you going?" she hissed, reaching for him as he climbed out.

"Stay here, please." Finn turned toward the SUV in question. "Lock the doors."

"Wait!" Hayley gasped as his door closed. She hit the automatic locks, then dialed 911 on her cell phone. She hovered her thumb over the screen, ready to send the call, and twisted in her seat to watch Finn move confidently away. Every horrific possibility charged through her mind as she braced for the pending encounter. Most involved bullets and blood.

The SUV launched forward with a bark of the tires.

Finn lurched sideways, thrown between parked cars.

"No!" The word tore from her throat in a scream as the SUV rocketed past her.

Hayley was on the sidewalk in an instant, racing toward Finn as the SUV rounded a corner behind her. Her sharp, pounding strides ate up the space between the truck and the location where Finn had disappeared. "Finn!"

A low moan slowed her steps.

He rose slowly off the concrete, from the space between parked cars. Palms bloody and arms rubbed raw from wrist to elbow. "Guess they didn't want to talk."

Her grip on the phone relaxed, and she burst forward, wrapping herself around him. "Oh, my goodness!" The force of her attack hug knocked him back against a busted Toyota. "You could've been killed!"

"Just a few scratches," he said, straightening to his full height, taking her with him. "I'm fine, but I'm getting blood on you."

She released him to better survey his physical damage. "I almost called 911."

"No need." He rolled his shoulders and tipped his head from side to side, stretching the muscles of his neck. "I don't suppose you got a look at the license plate?"

"I wasn't looking for a license plate." Her only thoughts had been of him. "I think you need to see a doctor. Maybe we should visit an urgent care before we keep going."

"I definitely don't need a doctor," he said, testing his fingers, wrists and elbows. Wincing with each move. "I couldn't see the driver. Too much sunlight reflecting on the windshield."

Hayley crossed her arms over her middle, hating that she'd thrown herself at him the way she had. Hating that whoever had tried to hit him would get away with it.

"Hey," he called, following her. "What's wrong?"

"You were nearly killed."

"I told you. I'm—"

She spun to glare at him. "Do not tell me you're fine."

Finn grinned. "Suit yourself."

She turned back to the truck, taking slow, deep breaths to regain her calm. She couldn't think about what would happen if she lost him. Even if she couldn't keep Finn in her life when this was over, the world was a better place with him in it.

Finn opened the driver's-side door and pulled a bottle of water from behind his seat. He unscrewed the lid and poured the contents over his hands and forearms, then used a towel from his gym bag to wipe away most of the blood. A few thin streams sprouted anew. “See? The rest of this will scab up by lunch. I don’t even need stitches.”

“Keep downplaying what just happened and you might need a few,” Hayley warned. She rounded the truck’s grill, reached the passenger’s door and climbed aboard.

Finn slid behind the wheel and started the engine. He pumped up the air-conditioning and pointed the vents in her direction. “I’m going to call this in before we move on,” he said. He tapped the vehicle’s dashboard screen while she buckled up.

Hayley swallowed a sudden wave of panic as he calmly relayed the details of his near death to someone at Marshal’s Bluff PD.

The voice on the other end of the line sounded distorted as heat climbed her neck and her ears began to ring. She leaned forward on her seat, fighting nausea and searching for oxygen.

Gage was missing. A killer wanted him dead. Parker was likely in tow.

And she thought she’d seen Finn mowed down by a Range Rover. Had imagined him never getting up again.

Her vision tunneled and she closed her eyes against the dark spots encroaching on her vision.

“Hayley.” Finn’s steady voice echoed in her ears. “Hey. Are you okay? Can you hear me?”

Her seat belt gave way with a snap, and Finn’s big hands curled around her biceps, dragging her toward him.

In the next moment she was across his lap, curled against his chest, face pressed to his neck. “Shh,” he said softly. “I’ve got you, and we’re both just fine. I promise.”

Hayley held on to his words like a lifeline as he stroked her back and gripped her tight. She pressed her palms to his chest and counted the beats of his heart until she was calm once more.

"Better?" he asked, not missing the release of tension in her body.

She raised her face to his, embarrassed at her unexpected reaction to the stress, infinitely thankful for his reaction to her. "I thought I lost you again."

His eyes darkened, and his lips parted. His gaze lowered to her mouth. "I'm right here."

Suddenly, every moment with him seemed so much more important than it had an hour before. This was it for her and Finn. They'd find Gage. Finn would arrest the killer. And the man she loved would be out of her life all over again. She hated the future, but she still had this moment.

Before she could talk herself out of it, she burrowed her fingers into the soft hair at the back of his head and urged his mouth to hers. She kissed him tenderly, hoping to convey how truly precious he was to her. She was desperate to show him all the things she hadn't found the courage to say.

And for one terrifying moment, Finn grew stone-still.

She dropped her hand away, pulling back in humiliation. "I am so sorry," she said in a rush, horrified by her unsolicited actions. "I didn't mean to—"

"Hayley." The deep rumble of pleasure in his chest had barely registered before his mouth returned to hers. The gentle sweep of his tongue sent fire through her veins, and the heady mix of joy and desire overtook her. She adjusted her body to better align with his, their hearts pounding together in a staccato rhythm.

"Ms. Campbell?" a deep male voice called, somewhat muffled by the closed windows.

A round of whoops and catcalls followed, returning her rudely to reality.

Hayley scrambled back to her side of the truck as a group of laughing teens came into view outside the windshield. She smoothed her hair as they closed in on the truck.

Finn stared at her, breathing heavy, his lips slightly swollen from her kisses. "Friends of yours?" Finn asked quietly, shifting his attention to the group.

"I only know the spokesman."

He powered down the window and set his bloody elbow across the frame.

"Ms. C?" A young man she recognized as Keith Shane, a former child from her caseload, frowned back. "What are you doing down here?" His attention flicked to Finn and his bloody arm, then back to her. "You okay?"

"Fine," she said, hoping to appear as if it was true and hating her word choice. She'd just yelled at Finn for saying the same thing. And like Finn, she was absolutely not fine. She'd just made out in the front seat of a truck in broad daylight. And been caught. She was supposed to be looking for two missing children. And behaving like a professional grown-up.

Keith crouched to stare boldly through the open window. "So what's going on in here?"

"This is Detective Beaumont," Hayley said, thankful her voice sounded natural and unbothered. "Detective, this is Keith."

The young man's brow rose briefly, then furrowed. His gaze hardened on the detective. "Did he bring you down here for a reason I need to know about?"

Her heart warmed at the kid's protective tone, and she smiled. "Actually, yes. We're looking for two boys. Parker and Gage, ages eight and fourteen. Gage is the artist who paints the shadow children on the buildings. Do you know him?"

The group behind Keith made a few comments in approval of the artwork. Keith took another long look at Finn before turning to confer with his friends.

"If you've seen either boy today," Finn said, voice thick with authority, "we need to know. We have reasons to believe both kids are in significant danger."

The group dragged their eyes from Finn to Hayley, apparently deciding what to do next.

"They aren't in any trouble," Hayley assured them. "I want to protect them, but first I need to find them."

A short, wiry guy in a plain white tank top and navy basketball shorts stepped forward. "I saw that kid at a rave." He glanced at Finn.

"We know about the rave," Finn said. "We know Gage was there. Someone was chasing him. Any chance you got a look at that person?"

The kid nodded. "Yeah, it was an old rich dude."

"How old?"

He shrugged. "I don't know. Thirty."

Hayley felt her breath catch. This was a new lead. "How did you know he was rich?"

"His clothes." The kid plucked the material of his tank top away from his chest. "He was bougie as hell. V-neck T-shirt. Three-hundred-dollar boat shoes. A watch I could hock to buy my ma a house."

"Ever seen him before that night?" she asked.

The kid shrugged. "Maybe. There's been a lot of folks like that around lately. Preparing for the community center, I guess. I figured your boy got caught taking something from him, or maybe he painted on the wrong building."

Finn straightened, giving up any final pretense of casual. "Anything else we should know?"

The teens commiserated. "Nah," Keith said, retaking his role as spokesman. "But I wouldn't worry. That guy never had a chance at catching him. Kids disappear down here for a lot of reasons. And if they don't want to be found, they won't be." The sad smile he offered Hayley implied that she could expect the same result.

She could only hope he was wrong. "Any idea where he calls home?" she asked.

The group traded looks then shook their heads.

Finn distributed his business cards. "If you see Gage or think of anything that can help us find and protect him, give me a call."

Hayley offered a composed smile. "I'm safe with the detective," she said, noting the lingering concern in Keith's eyes. "He's one of the good ones."

Keith nodded in acceptance, then led his friends away.

Finn powered up the window and set his hands on the wheel. "Well, that was—"

"Embarrassing? Humiliating? Awful?" Hayley offered, feeling latent heat rise over her cheeks.

"I was going to say lucky," Finn said. "Based on his description, we can assume I was right in theorizing that Kate's killer wasn't robbing her. People in expensive shoes don't come down here at night if they can avoid it. They certainly don't chase kids into raves without serious motivation."

"Like getting away with murder," she mused.

"Yep." He shifted the truck into gear and headed deeper into Old Downtown.

Chapter Fourteen

Hayley tried not to obsess over the kiss. She'd acted impulsively but didn't regret it. And he'd kissed her back. Good and right. Her toes curled inside her shoes at the memory. The timing, location and audience were severely unfortunate, but damn…

Had it been more than just heightened emotions that had caused Finn to return the affection? He'd yet to comment on her tearful confession the night before. Not that they'd had time to talk about anything other than Gage and Parker today.

Finn turned onto the street where the rave had taken place and Kate's body had been discovered. The hour was early, and they'd yet to see anyone other than Keith and his friends.

She wet her still tingling lips and pushed aside thoughts of personal problems. Something more important suddenly had her attention. "Do you see all these signs?" she asked. "I didn't notice them when we were here before."

Rectangles of sturdy white cardboard had been affixed to multiple buildings in the area, each marked with the logo of an unfamiliar company.

"Is that an investment group?" he asked.

"Maybe. I've never heard of Lighthouse, Inc. Is it one of Kate's companies?"

"I'm not sure," he said, parking the truck once more. "What do you think about taking another look at the warehouse where the old rich guy was seen?" He smiled. "I want to be sure we didn't miss anything there."

Hayley agreed and followed him out of the truck, then into the site of the rave. Empty plastic bags and sheets of newspapers blew over the silent, empty street as they entered. Their footfalls echoed in the stillness.

"Stay close," he said, posture tense, clearly on high alert.

She easily complied.

Dust motes sparkled like silver confetti in shafts of sunlight through broken windows. Sounds of the distant sea rose through the missing rear wall to her ears. A Lighthouse, Inc. sign on the broken boards drew her eyes. "Look."

They moved to the back, approaching the sign for inspection.

"Condemned," Finn read. "Marked for demolition. Unsafe for inhabitants and industry." He snapped a photo of the large cardboard warning then tapped his phone screen. "Let's see what Dean can learn about the company."

"They seem to own everything nearby," Hayley said. That had to mean something. "Maybe Lighthouse, Inc. is involved in the community-center project somehow."

Finn stilled. He worked his jaw and slid his gaze over the space around them, posture stiffening incrementally.

Hayley followed his eyes, searching for what had gotten his attention, but seeing nothing unusual. "What is it?"

"I'm not sure." His phone rang, and she started. "Hey," he answered, raising the device to his ear. "We're at the warehouse now—"

The sounds of squealing tires and rapid gunfire erupted from the world outside.

Splinters of wood burst into the air around them, and a

scream ripped from Hayley's throat. Finn's body collided with hers in the next heartbeat, jolting them forward.

"Run!" he hollered, thrusting her toward the missing back wall, where nothing stood between them and the sea far below.

"But—" Something bounced and rolled in her peripheral vision as the car roared away, and she recognized the urgency. "Is that dynamite?" she screeched.

Finn jerked her by the wrist, forcing her into a sprint. "Jump!" he yelled a moment before they launched into the air.

Her feet left the warehouse floorboards, bicycling high above the sea.

Their joint freefall began as the warehouse exploded.

Another scream ripped from Hayley. Her ears rang and her vision blurred with the intensity of the boom.

Debris blew into the sky around them. Bits of busted stone and chunks of roofing. Clods of earth and fractured beams. A thousand pieces of instant shrapnel. Some sliced her clothes and others bit her skin.

Then, it was all swallowed by harbor water.

The impact pushed the air from her lungs. Shock separated her mind and limbs, leaving her body to twist and roll helplessly in the dark silence of the sea. She searched for the surface, fighting the pitch and heave of undercurrents, burning with need for oxygen.

Would she survive an explosion only to drown in the waters below?

Demanding hands gripped her waist in the next moment, propelling her upward. She recognized Finn's touch before she saw him. Before she took her next breath.

Her mouth opened and her body gasped as they broke the surface—she pulled sweet salt air deep into her lungs.

"I've got you," he promised, between the raspy breaths and the rhythmic kicking of his legs. "Are you okay?" he asked, treading water as he caressed her cheek and scanned her face with worried eyes.

She opened her mouth to speak, but a fit of coughing erupted instead. Followed by a stomach full of salt water. How much had she swallowed?

Finn pulled her against his chest and began an awkward backstroke toward the shore.

Emergency sirens wailed in the distance, growing louder and more fervent with each inch of progress Finn made.

He towed her through a floating field of charred and busted planks, dodging the larger, most ragged pieces. "Only a little farther," he promised, his breaths coming rougher and shorter.

Slowly, Hayley's mind and body reunited, coordinating her limbs. She helped him paddle until his feet struck the ground below.

"Help is on the way," he panted, setting her gingerly on the rocky shore. "They'll be here soon."

She took a mental inventory of her faculties and scanned her body for injuries. All her parts were accounted for, and the cuts and bruises were shockingly few. Though she'd still have been dead, if not for Finn. "You saved my life."

He dipped his chin in acknowledgement, eyes scanning the top of the hill, where a cluster of onlookers had appeared. Blood lined his mouth, seeping from a split in his lip, and a large purple knot had formed beside his right eye.

"You're hurt." She reached for his hands, pulling him down, certain her shaking legs wouldn't hold her if she tried to stand. "Sit. It could be bad. Adrenaline can cover serious injuries."

He wobbled slightly, then fell to his knees, his body stiff

as he winced. His shirt was torn and his arms were bleeding. Suddenly, the scrapes from the earlier road incident seemed like paper cuts in comparison.

Hayley's gaze shot to the warehouse on the hill, or what remained of it. The explosion had demolished the back half, reducing that portion of the structure to rubble. *Exactly what dynamite tended to do*, she thought. And they'd been inside moments before it blew. She sucked a ragged breath as something horrendous came to mind. "What if—" The words were lodged in her throat, unable to break free.

What if Gage and Parker had been there too?

"We were alone," Finn said, offering comfort and apparently reading her mind. He eased into the space beside her then reached for her trembling hands.

"Someone blew up a building to kill us," she said. The words were nonsensical. How could anything so outrageous be true?

Finn gave her fingers a squeeze. "I'm guessing they used C-4 from a nearby construction site, and the one who threw the explosive was probably the same person driving the SUV that nearly hit me." His normally tanned skin was unusually white, and his gaze slightly unfocused.

"I think you should lay back," Hayley said. "You're going to need stitches. I don't know how much blood you've lost. Or if you have other injuries. Did anything hit your head as we fell?" There had been a lot of large debris, and he'd used his body to protect her.

"I'm all right," he said. "Just wondering what's taking the ambulance so long."

"There they are!" someone called from the top of the hill, drawing Hayley's eyes back to the growing crowd. She waved a limp arm overhead.

"Help is coming!" a stranger called. "They're almost here!"

"I can't believe they're alive!" someone else yelled. "That place blew into splinters!"

Finn slumped against Hayley's side, and she wound an arm around him. Hopefully, the crowd was enough deterrent to keep their near-assassin from taking another shot. Neither she nor Finn were in any condition to run again. She wasn't convinced they were even ready to stand.

A collection of rocks and dirt slid over the hill in their direction, accompanied by a pair of EMTs. The men wore matching uniforms and expressions of disbelief while carrying backboards and medical kits.

Hayley knew exactly how they felt.

A long hour later, she and Finn were sequestered in side-by-side ambulances. Hayley's EMT had examined her swiftly, cleaned her wounds, then hooked her up to an IV to replenish lost fluids.

Outside the open bay doors, uniformed officers interviewed the crowd. From what she could piece together, several people had heard the squealing tires that preceded the dynamite delivery, but no one had seen the car causing all the noise or its driver.

Finn strode into view, scowling, with an EMT trailing behind.

"Detective," the medic pleaded. "I haven't finished." He swiped an alcohol pad over the back of Finn's arm as they moved.

"Yes," Finn corrected. "You have. I appreciated the IV and bandages. The rest of this will heal on its own."

Hayley smiled despite herself. "You should go to the hospital and let them check you more thoroughly," she said, watching as he climbed aboard with her.

"I'm fine. I wasn't hit by anything big, and I've cliff-dived from greater heights. I got a little dinged up, but it's been handled. What about you?"

"Oh, I'm super," she said, struggling to maintain her smile. Images of Finn cliff-diving helped. She wished she could've been there to see him make a leap like that for fun.

He looked to the EMT for confirmation. "She's okay?"

"She's going to heal completely, with rest and fluids," the man said. "For the record, I don't think either of you are okay. That was quite an experience. You both need to take a few days and rest. Visible wounds or not."

"Noted," Finn said, though he didn't look convinced. He looked like a losing prizefighter. His split lip had swollen, and the knot on his head had grown. "If we're cleared to go, I think we're ready."

Hayley nodded in agreement when he turned her way.

The EMT sighed and removed Hayley's IV. "Fluids and rest," he repeated. "Something over-the-counter for pain."

"Thank you." Hayley waved. She let Finn help her down from the ambulance then along the sidewalk to his truck on the next block.

The day was insufferably hot, the air thick with stifling humidity. A secondary crowd had gathered outside the warehouse remains.

She recognized Dean on the outskirts surveying the scene.

Finn unlocked the pickup as they approached, and Hayley climbed inside.

Her previously soaked clothes were wrinkled and dirty, and had been dried by the relentless heat. She peeled strands of tangled hair from her cheeks and neck. "Are you sure you're okay?" she asked.

"Physically, sure," he said. "But I've been wondering

how long we were followed." He eased behind the wheel with a small wince. "Some of what we said after leaving the truck might've been overheard. Maybe even our chat with Keith and his friends."

Hayley tensed, thinking about all the things she'd spoken with Finn about in the time before the explosion. "Someone could know we're looking for the spot Gage called home. They'll be looking for it too."

Finn shifted into gear and piloted the vehicle back toward town, scanning pedestrians and passing traffic with care. "Gage's file mentioned active involvement at his middle school last year. Band. Soccer. Art camps. His parents led a few extracurriculars as well. Let's start there, and see if there's any place he could make a temporary home. Somewhere to relive the better days."

"He attended Virginia Dare middle school," Hayley said. She reached for her phone before remembering it was at the bottom of the bay. "He was part of the swim team too, and I think there's a pool on the property."

Finn stretched across the cab and opened the glove box. He withdrew a handgun and cell phone. "Do you remember the address of his home?"

She searched her memory for the information but came up empty. "No. I'm sorry."

"Would you mind giving your office a call? Asking someone to look in the file?"

She took the device with trembling fingers, and Finn made the next turn toward the middle school. By the time they arrived, she'd gained the information they needed, and Finn had passed it on to his team.

"I'll ask Dispatch to send a cruiser to the house and talk to the new owners," he said. "We'll let them know there's a possibility a couple of kids might show up, try to sleep in the backyard playhouse or elsewhere on the grounds. If that happens, the owners can give the station a call."

Hayley wiped tears from her cheeks, unsure what had prompted them this time.

"You doing okay?" Finn asked.

She shook her head, unable to lie. "I thought I was tough, but this whole situation has been awful. How do you do this every day?"

Finn smiled kindly. "This isn't a typical workweek," he said. "I'm not usually in continual danger, and the good I do is always worth the trouble. I'm sorry you're in the line of fire this week. If I could change that, I would."

"Don't feel too badly," she said. "I brought the fire."

Finn chose a spot in the middle-school parking lot, then turned stormy eyes on her.

A cascade of goose bumps scattered over her skin in the quiet cab, and her lips parted of their own accord. "I kissed you," she whispered. Somehow, that had been the least dangerous yet most traumatic event to occur since breakfast.

Maybe the timing was wrong, but she'd bared her heart to him in words last night and in actions this morning. She needed to know where he stood on the matter. She needed to settle at least this one thing in a time when everything else was beyond her reach. She had no means of getting answers to Gage's whereabouts. Or Parker's. Had no way of knowing who'd killed Kate and wanted to kill her too. But she could ask Finn to be direct with her, and she could get this one issue solved.

"We should talk about that when this is over," he said, turning his attention to something beyond the truck's window. "Looks like the groundskeeper is headed our way."

She followed Finn's gaze to a man in jeans and a navy blue T-shirt with the school's logo.

Grass clippings stuck to the bottoms of his pant legs and a curious look crossed his heavily creased face. He grinned as he drew near. "Finn Beaumont. What brings you around here? How's your family doing?"

Finn climbed out and met the man on the passenger's side. He shook his hand.

Hayley powered down her window, hoping to hide her aching limbs and frazzled nerves by remaining inside the truck.

"Nice to see you again, Eric," Finn said. "The family's good. This is Hayley Campbell. She's a social worker, and we're looking for a former student. He's in foster care now, attending the high school this year. He's gone missing. Runaway, we believe. We're hoping you might be able to help."

The older man accepted the handshake then crossed his arms and listened intently as Finn covered the important details of Gage's story. Eric removed his hat when Finn finished. "I remember Gage. Remember the accident. Hell, I remember his folks. Nice, good people. What happened to them was unthinkable. Our whole community grieved. I hate to hear he's taken off, but his world must be in a shambles."

Hayley nearly choked at the painful understatement. Eric didn't know the half of it. She passed a business card through the open window and into his hand. "If you see him, will you reach out to the police or call me directly?"

"Will do." Eric raised two fingers to his forehead, saluting them as Finn retook his seat behind the wheel and shifted into Reverse.

Hayley sent out another round of prayers to the universe as they motored away.

Let us find those boys before the killer can.

Chapter Fifteen

Hayley tried and failed to rest all afternoon. Her body was sore and fatigued, but her mind was in overdrive. She'd nearly died today while under the protection of a lawman. What chance did Gage have at survival on his own while caring for a kid?

Finn's brothers and other detectives had visited the pool where Gage used to swim, along with a few other spots from the teen's past, but none had revealed any indication the boys had been there.

Meanwhile, Finn and Hayley had returned to his house. Mrs. Beaumont had delivered a delicious lunch, and Hayley had taken a lengthy, indulgent shower, but her tension only increased. She couldn't shake the sensation a giant clock was counting down, and the boys were running out of time.

She dragged Finn's laptop onto the couch with her while he took his turn in the shower. If she couldn't be on the streets searching for Gage and Parker, she could at least keep looking for clues online. She started with the name of the company that had plastered signs all over Old Downtown.

Her initial findings revealed Lighthouse, Inc. to be a small company located in Marshal's Bluff. Real-estate projects seemed to be the business's focus, but it was unclear if Lighthouse, Inc. was an investment group or something else. The website was static, and the accompanying social-media accounts were sorely lacking.

Sounds of the shower filtered to her ears, and Hayley did her best to ignore them. In the big scheme of her current problems, matters of the heart should've been less than irrelevant. But knowing Finn was naked and separated from her by one closed door made it unreasonably hard to concentrate.

She clicked the next link on her web search, and an image of Kate pulled her focus back to where it belonged. The article featured the philanthropist as the keynote speaker at a recent fundraising gala. The caption below the photo identified her and the men at her side. Her husband, Topper, and Conrad Forester, the CEO of Lighthouse, Inc.

Hayley swung her feet onto the floor and opened another browser window, starting a second search. She added Kate and her husband's names to the words *Lighthouse, Inc.* Several links appeared. Each time, the results also mentioned Conrad Forester. Apparently, the trio had golfed together, boated together and attended a number of other community events.

Did they simply run in the same circles, or were they friends outside their work? The three of them? Or only two? If the latter, then who was the third wheel? More importantly, was their connection relevant to the case?

The water shut off in the bathroom, and Hayley rose to her feet. She paced the carpeted space between the couch and hallway, waiting for Finn to appear. She wasn't a detective, but something inside her told her this new knowledge mattered. Finn would know for sure.

When the door opened and he emerged in a clingy T-shirt

and cloud of Finn-scented steam, she allowed herself a moment to appreciate the view.

Her eyes met his a heartbeat later, and his mischievous grin suggested he'd noticed exactly how long it'd taken her to pull herself together. "What's up?" he asked, rubbing a towel over damp, tousled hair.

"I think I found something." She pointed over her shoulder, refusing to steal another glance at his nicely curved biceps as he draped the towel around his neck.

"What is it?"

She returned to the couch and passed him the laptop, recapping her concern.

"That is interesting," he agreed. "It makes sense a company involved in real estate would know her. Their work probably brought them together from time to time. The frequent interactions could've made them friends."

"Do you think they were collaborating on the community-center project?"

Finn grinned. "I can think of one way to find out. How are you feeling?"

"Like I could sleep until retirement, but I'm too wound up to rest."

Finn checked his watch. "If we hurry, we might catch Mr. Forester at work before office hours end."

"Then we'd better get moving."

LIGHTHOUSE, INC. WAS housed in a single-story cottage in the shopping district. The former residential property was covered in gray-blue vinyl siding and trimmed in white. A small porch with two steps and a coordinating black handrail matched the roof and front door. According to the sign in the window, the office was open.

Finn held the door for Hayley. "After you."

Seashell wind chimes jangled overhead as she crossed the threshold.

"May I help you?" a young woman in a periwinkle-blue sundress asked. Her long brown hair hung in waves across her shoulders. The welcome desk where she sat was white and tidy, topped with a keyboard and monitor.

Finn raised his detective shield. "We're here to speak with Conrad Forester."

Her eyes widened in response. She looked from Finn to Hayley, then to a set of closed doors on the far wall before managing to recover. "Do you have an appointment?"

Finn wiggled the badge. "Yep."

She nodded shakily. "Right." She turned her focus to the monitor and typed something with her keyboard.

Hayley gave the office a more thorough look while they waited. A small sitting area beside the welcome desk held a couch, a set of armchairs and a coffee table covered in boating magazines. A placard on one of the closed doors across the room identified it as a restroom. The others, Hayley presumed, were offices.

"He'll be right out," the woman said.

Finn turned to stare at the closed doors, ignoring the comfortable-looking couch and armchairs. Hayley followed his lead.

Soon, one of the doors opened, and a tall, broad-shouldered man stepped out. "Detective."

"Mr. Forester," Finn said, approaching for a handshake. "This is Hayley Campbell."

"Good afternoon." Mr. Forester offered her a plaintive smile. His face was tan and his forehead lined with creases. A sprinkle of gray touched his otherwise sandy hair. He didn't invite them in. "What can I do for you?" he asked, swinging troubled brown eyes back to Finn.

"I'm looking into the murder of Katherine Everett," Finn said.

Mr. Forester nodded solemnly. "A true shame. She'll be greatly missed in this community."

"Couldn't agree more," Finn said. "I also couldn't help noticing signs for your company all over the area where her body was discovered."

The soft sounds of typing ceased, and Hayley fought the urge to look at the woman who'd welcomed them. Instead, she kept her eyes on the man before her, as he seemed to pale at the mention of his company signs in conjunction with Kate's murder.

"We're planning to improve the area near the bay," Forester said. "The changes will bring in local businesses, reduce crime, create condos along the waterfront and single-family homes along the fringe. Parks. Playgrounds. The whole deal." His smile grew as he spoke, and his demeanor became congenial. As if he was reciting a canned pitch for the media or as a marketing speech, not explaining himself to a detective investigating a homicide.

Hayley struggled to keep her expression blank and guarded.

"Condos," Finn repeated, the disbelief in the single word making it fall flat. "In Old Downtown."

She understood the skepticism. The area in question was too raw and riddled with trouble. The criminal population alone would likely destroy or make off with any decent building materials before the things on Forester's list ever came to fruition.

Creating a community center and homeless shelter in an area was one thing. The people and the area were in desperate need of love and housing. Replacing everything with high-end housing and businesses was rubbing salt in a proverbial wound.

"Shopping too," Forester said. "Pubs, cafés, jobs. Whatever it takes to get families down that way."

Finn stared at him, silently scrutinizing. Hayley would've confessed to anything if she'd been on the other side of that look, but Forester kept up the unbothered grin. "How well did you know Katherine Everett?" Finn asked.

Forester rocked back on his heels. "Not well." He put his palms in front of him. "We weren't strangers, but we were friendly enough to say hello when we crossed paths."

"That happened a lot," Finn said. "I understand the two of you were friends. You did a number of things together. Boating. Golfing. Charity events and whatnot."

"Well." Forester chuckled. "That's what business owners do, isn't it? We lend a hand however we can. Golf outings, nautical events, dinners—they're all for a cause."

Finn sucked his teeth. "So you didn't have a personal relationship with Kate or her husband?"

Forester's smile slipped by a fraction. A ringing phone drew his attention through the open door behind him. "I'm sorry to do this, but I've been expecting that call. Would you mind?"

"Not at all," Finn said. "I'll be in touch if I need anything else."

Forester took his leave, pulling the door closed in his wake.

Hayley waved to the woman at the welcome desk on her way out, then they hurried back to Finn's truck. "Are you thinking what I'm thinking?" she asked.

"Depends." Finn opened the door and waited while she climbed inside. "Are you thinking he seemed extremely on edge beneath the forced smile?"

"Yeah, and I'm guessing Kate's plans would've put a big dent in the value of his condos."

FINN STRETCHED HIS aching limbs into cotton joggers and an old concert T-shirt later that evening, thankful for the rest of the night off. His team at Marshal's Bluff PD was working around the clock to find the missing boys and put the pieces of Kate's murder investigation together. Finn had no doubt they'd be in touch if anything significant came to light. Meanwhile, he needed to recuperate. He'd barely had the energy to visit with his mom and shower after the explosion. The trip to Lighthouse, Inc. had put him over the edge. But there was still one more thing he needed to do. Having a talk with Hayley about her confession the previous night, and their kiss earlier today, was already overdue.

He'd originally imagined her reason for confiding in him was simply to clear the air so they could move forward as friends. Especially since they'd become impromptu roommates. The kiss they'd shared, however, made him wonder if there was hope for more. It wasn't uncommon for people under extreme stress to find physical outlets, and all the things they'd been through certainly qualified as stressful, but he wanted to hear it from Hayley. Was her behavior a result of heightened emotions, or was there a chance they could find their way back to one another? He'd never forgive himself if the case ended, and she walked away because he hadn't taken the opportunity to set things straight while he had a chance.

Finn inhaled deeply, then released the breath slowly. He'd dreamed of being in Hayley's life again, and now she was living under his roof, sharing his meals and at his side in every moment of the day. He didn't want to screw that up or scare her away again. Whatever happened between them, he'd never stop protecting her in any way he could.

His eyes found her as he moved down the hall toward the living room. She looked like his personal heaven curled on the couch in a messy bun, oversize shirt and sleep shorts. She was so much more than a beautiful woman, human and friend. She was the place he wanted to get lost in, but he didn't have that luxury. Not while two boys were missing and a killer was at large. Hell, he wasn't sure he had that option at all. But it was time he and Hayley figured that out.

"Hey." She smiled as he entered the room. "How are you feeling?"

"Like I was in an explosion." He stopped in the kitchen and pulled two bottles from the fridge, then lifted them in question.

"Yes, please." Her eyes traveled the length of his arms and neck, pausing briefly on every cut, scrape and bandage, then on his swollen eye. "You look terrible."

"I feel terrible. How about you? You doing okay?"

Hayley pulled her bottom lip between her teeth. "I'm still hoping you want to talk." The blush creeping over her lightly freckled cheeks said she'd been thinking about her confession and their recent kiss as well.

Finn carried the bottles of water to the coffee table and took a seat on the couch beside her. She moved closer, leaning in and fitting perfectly against his side. He released a contented sigh and let his arm curve around her. This could've been their life.

If he'd gone after her that night.

If she'd found her voice sooner.

If he'd seen the signs of her pain and asked about them.

If he'd had a clue.

"Finn?"

He shook away the what-ifs and angled his head toward her, resting his chin atop her crown. "Yeah?"

"I hate that all of this is happening, but I'm glad you're here. We're alive today because of you."

He stroked her soft hair and inhaled her sweet scent, unsure of what to say. His every action today, and every day since she'd shown up unexpectedly in his office, were born of instinct and a bone-deep need to protect her at any cost. "You will always be safe with me," he promised.

"I know." She pulled away to look into his eyes. "I'm sorry I lost it last night when I was explaining myself. I wanted you to know all those things, but I didn't expect to be flooded with emotion while I shared. I definitely didn't think I'd be so embarrassed by the outburst I'd cry myself to sleep."

"You never have to be embarrassed with me," he said softly, meaning it to his core. "You can always tell me anything."

She gave a sad laugh. "I left you without an explanation last year. Then I dumped the whole story on you last night and left again. This is not who I'm trying to be."

Her words drew a small smile over his face.

"I know who you are, Hayley Campbell," he stated simply, stroking the backs of his fingers across her cheek. "I wish I'd known about your pain sooner, but I'm glad you told me. A lot of things make more sense now. And because I know, I can be more aware and sensitive to you."

"Do you have any questions?" she asked, gaze darting away then back. "I can try to fill in any blanks I left."

Finn opened his mouth to say he'd listen to anything she wanted to tell him, but he wouldn't pry. Instead, a different set of words rolled off his tongue. "Why'd you kiss me today?"

Hayley froze in his arms and pulled in a deep breath. "I thought you'd been hit by that car. The possibility I'd lost you again, forever and for real this time, was gutting. I never want to live in that reality. Even if you never speak to me again after this case ends, I need to know you're okay and happy somewhere. Nothing else makes any sense. You know?"

He pulled her against his chest and held her a little more tightly, because he knew exactly what she meant.

Chapter Sixteen

Hayley forced herself to push away from Finn's protective hold. She had more to say and needed to get it out before the phone rang or someone else tried to kill them. She tucked her feet beneath her and angled to face him on the cushions. "I want you to know I'm committed to healing. I don't want to hurt anymore, and I don't want to hurt anyone else like I hurt you. It's been a long road just getting this far, but I won't quit. I still meet with my therapist weekly to sort through the thoughts and feelings that make me feel unlovable. I have no intention of going back to where I was last year."

His kind eyes crinkled at the corners and he tipped his head slightly. Interest and something that looked a lot like pride flashed in his expression. "I believe you. Do you want to talk about it?"

She shifted, debating, but knew she needed to be brave and honest. "A little."

Finn nodded, holding her gaze. Then he waited patiently while she gathered the right words to continue.

"So far my key takeaways have been that my mother is an alcoholic. She has been for the majority of my life, and she will always be. She doesn't accept this as truth, and she is nowhere near the point of seeking help. Her behavior isn't my fault, and there's nothing I could've done better that would've changed her choices or healed her illness. She has to do that herself. I tried talking to her about it over dinner last fall, but she accused me of making slanderous accusations to hurt her."

Hayley took another steadying breath and swallowed, determined not to cry again. "I've accepted that my childhood was a series of minor and major abuses, and that I've both survived and thrived as a human despite her. Those unfortunate experiences have shaped and burdened every relationship I've had, including what I had with you. I'm distrustful and needy. Desperate to help others while neglecting myself. And a whole slew of other opposing concepts that keep me unsettled. But I'm working on those too." She pressed her lips together. "I will not pretend everything is fine like my mother."

Finn set a hand over hers as he'd done so many times before, an offer of shared strength. "How often do you get to see or speak to your mother now?" Finn asked, cutting to the quick of Hayley's pain. Seeing the thing she hadn't been able to say.

"I don't. Not since that dinner last year." Because until Hayley fully healed, interacting with her mother would only destroy the progress she'd fought so hard to make. She waited for Finn to say more, then tensed with each passing breath in silence. "What are you thinking?"

"I'm thinking that you used self-sabotage to avoid happiness," he said.

"I did."

"That's not uncommon when you spent so long being miserable."

Hayley nodded, thankful for the millionth time that Finn understood but never judged. "I should've trusted you with all of this sooner." She'd known in her heart that he wasn't like the others who'd hurt her, but her instinct had still been to run.

Finn opened his arms and raised his chin, coaxing her closer. She fell against him, immediately cocooned in his embrace.

"I'm broken in so many ways," she whispered.

"You are healing in far more." He pulled her onto his lap and pressed a kiss to the top of her head. "I'm glad you're on this path," he said softly. "You deserve happiness, Hayley. You deserve the world."

She tipped her head away for a view of his sincere brown eyes. "What if the only thing I've wanted in a very long time is you, and I ruined it?"

Finn's gaze darkened, and he lifted a palm to cradle her jaw. One strong thumb stroked her cheek. "I'm right here, just like I always have been. Like I always will be."

Her gaze dropped to his lips, and he angled his mouth to hers in response. The delicious scent of him encompassed her. The heat of his skin and tantalizing pressure of his embrace was instant ecstasy. When the kiss deepened and their tongues met in that perfect, familiar, sensual slide, she knew she'd finally come home.

Hayley woke on the couch in Finn's arms the next morning. A call from his team roused them both from a deep slumber. It was the first truly good night of rest Hayley had had since the mess with Gage first began. Finn appeared astonished at the sight of the clock. She assumed he was feeling the same way.

An hour later, like the days before, they were up and out the door. Hastily dressed in denim capris, black flats and a white silk tank, she sat beside him in his pickup as they approached Katherine Everett's home. They rolled along the winding paved driveway that stretched between a posh gated entrance and the massive brick estate. The experience was a little like traveling to another world. “I had no idea homes like this existed in Marshal’s Bluff,” Hayley said, leaning forward to drink in the views. Majestic oaks lined the path, their gnarled, moss-soaked limbs stretching overhead, the road before them dappled in golden light.

“There are a few,” he said. “And there are usually lawyers waiting for me when I visit.”

She wrinkled her nose. “Frustrating.”

Finn piloted the truck around a stone fountain outside the sprawling estate and parked near a sleek Mercedes convertible. He inhaled deeply, perhaps preparing himself for those lawyers. Then he opened his door.

Hayley followed suit and met him at the fountain, where they exchanged small smiles.

“You should get one,” she teased. “Your yard chickens would love it.”

Finn snorted before schooling his features into detective mode and leading the way to the home’s front doors. He rang the bell and scanned the structure while he waited.

Hayley tried not to gawk as she admired the detail work along the eaves, around the windows and in the stylized shrubbery. Katherine Everett had always appeared so casual and down-to-earth online and during her television interviews. No different than those she helped. Clearly, that had been a mask.

Finn pressed the bell a second time and shifted for a peek through the beveled glass.

“Are you sure he’s home?” Hayley asked. They’d come without calling after all.

“I believe that’s his car of choice,” Finn said, nodding toward the convertible. “One of a dozen registered in his name. Plus, it's still fairly early, and given his recent loss, I'd expect a husband to be taking time off from whatever he does to grieve."

"What does he do?" Hayley asked, realizing she had no idea. Was being the spouse of Kate enough to keep a person busy?

Finn's eyebrows tented. "Not much as far as I can tell."

The door opened, sweeping her attention to a woman in black slacks and a crimson blouse. "May I help you?"

Finn flashed his badge and her lips turned down in distaste.

"The police have already been here to speak with Mr. Everett," she said, coolly. "I'm sure they have everything they need, and Mr. Everett's attorney's contact information for future inquiries."

Finn stepped toward her, causing her to step back. "I won't keep him long. I understand this is a sensitive time for Mr. Everett, but I'm sure he's as interested in finding his wife's killer as I am. Would you mind letting him know I'm here?"

The woman pulled her chin back and balked.

"My name is Detective Beaumont."

She turned with a huff. "I'll see if Mr. Everett is available." She left the front door open and stormed into the home.

Finn waited for Hayley to step into the foyer, then he followed the woman across acres of Italian marble and through sliding glass doors to a rear patio.

Hayley hurried along in their wake, devouring the delicious interior views. Each space she passed looked more like an image from a design magazine than the last. As if Pinterest had exploded and all the pieces landed in one magnificent array for the Everetts to enjoy.

She stole one last peek at the mind-bending gourmet kitchen before stepping back into the scorching summer heat.

It took a moment for her eyes to adjust as sunlight glinted off the water of an impressive in-ground pool. Gorgeous tropical-looking plants and landscaping ran the length of the space between home and cabana. An outdoor kitchen, bar, fireplace and rocky waterfall feature filled the area nearest a hot tub. Finn and the woman stopped short of the bubbling water, where a shirtless man was sitting chest-deep.

Mirrored sunglasses covered his eyes as he sipped from a tall glass. A few soft words were exchanged, and he rose, revealing orange board shorts and the physique of a significantly younger man. If not for the thinning gray hair, Mr. Everett might've been in his late thirties instead of his early fifties. Perhaps that answered the question of what he did all day as Kate's husband. Clearly, he worked out.

The woman presented him with a large striped beach towel, and he wrapped it around his waist.

"This way," she said, flipping her wrist as she passed Hayley near the patio doors. "You can wait in the study."

Finn slowed at her side and set a hand against the small of her back as they reentered the home. A few footsteps later, they arrived at a fancy office Hayley had noticed on her way through.

An executive desk the size of an elephant centered the room and mahogany bookshelves climbed from floor to ceiling along the back wall. Matching leather armchairs faced the perfectly clean desk. A single framed photo of Kate and the man from the hot tub adorned the glossy wooden surface. They appeared happy on a boat at sea.

"Wait here," the woman said, then pulled the tall double doors shut behind her.

Finn circled the room's periphery without speaking, and

Hayley took a seat in an armchair. Something about the space made her think they might be on camera. The room was too pristine to be anyone's real office, too staged to be used as more than a prop.

This was most likely the enhanced, if not blatantly false, image Mr. Everett wanted people to believe of him, Hayley realized. A middle-aged man's push-up bra and French tips. The idea only made her more curious about who he truly was.

The doors reopened, and the man from the hot tub entered. The sunglasses were gone, as were the board shorts. Now, he had on navy dress shorts with boat shoes and a salmon-pink polo shirt with a designer insignia on the collar. She couldn't help wondering if his shoes were the same ones Keith's friend had seen on the man chasing Gage through the rave.

"Mr. Everett," Finn said, offering his hand. "Thank you for seeing me."

Kate's husband nodded, frowning. "Of course. Call me Topper. Please make yourself at home."

Finn took the seat beside Hayley's, clearly unimpressed. "This is Hayley Campbell, a local social worker interested in your wife's project."

She smiled. Mr. Everett did not.

"What can I do for you today, Detective?" he asked, moving to the seat behind the large desk. "You have news on my wife's case?"

"A bit, yes." Finn angled forward, pinning the other man with an inscrutable cop stare. "I was hoping you could tell me about Lighthouse, Inc."

Mr. Everett leaned away, causing the spring in his chair to squeak. His eyes narrowed, as if he was deep in thought. "I believe they've worked with my wife on various projects of the past."

"What about her community center in Old Downtown?" Finn asked.

"I couldn't say." Mr. Everett's gaze roamed to the grandfather clock beside his window, to the ceiling and then to Hayley, before returning to Finn. "Kate had a number of things in motion all the time. No one could keep up." He forced a pitiful smile. "She was a force."

"Agreed," Finn said. "What can you tell me about Lighthouse, Inc. in general?"

"It's a local business."

"Investors?" Finn asked.

"Land developers, I believe."

"How well do you know the owners of the company?"

Hayley let her attention bounce from Finn to Mr. Everett and back, nerves tightening.

"We're acquainted," Mr. Everett hedged, swaying forward once more. He anchored his forearms on the desk and laced his fingers.

"I see. How did you meet, initially?"

"Conrad is a member of Ardent Lakes."

"Conrad Forester," Finn clarified.

"Yes."

Hayley recognized Ardent Lakes as the name of a local country club. She'd driven past the gates a hundred times, but had never been inside. "Mr. Everett," she said, pulling both men's attention to her. "Sorry to interrupt, but I'm wondering about the community center." She'd been introduced as a social worker. She might as well play her role. "A great many people will benefit from the completed project. I hope it will continue. In your wife's honor, perhaps?"

Everett cleared his throat. "As I mentioned, I don't typically get involved in Kate's work, so I can't say what will happen now. I suppose that will be at the discretion of the board of trustees." His attention flickered to the clock again, then back to Finn. "I hate to rush you, but I have somewhere I need to be." He rose and pulled a set of car keys from his pocket as if in evidence.

"Of course." Finn pressed onto his feet and offered his hand once more in a farewell shake. "Thank you for your time. I'll be in touch if I need anything else."

Mr. Everett hurried ahead of them to the office door, then opened it and walked with them outside. He boarded the little blue car while she and Finn loaded into the truck.

She glanced in the rearview mirror as they motored down the lane, their pickup leading thc way. Her eyes fixed on the strange man behind them. "That was weird, right?"

"Yup."

"Do you think he's hiding something?"

Everett's thinning brown hair lifted on the breeze, eyes hidden behind those darn sunglasses once more.

"Probably," Finn said.

"Do you think he killed her?"

"Statistically, the odds aren't in his favor," Finn said. "Realistically, I don't know. Could be he's just glad to inherit the kingdom. Everybody's hiding something, but most of the things we get squirrelly about as individuals are irrelevant outside our heads."

She relaxed against the sun-warmed seat back, certainly able to relate. "Should we visit the country club next?" she asked. "Or maybe drive past a few parks and look for the boys?"

Finn slowed at the end of the driveway, checking both directions and signaling his turn for the man behind them. "We can do all of that if you're up to it. The day's still young."

The sound of squealing tires on pavement turned Hayley's eyes away from Finn. Her heart lurched into a sprint as the black SUV from Old Downtown raced along the street in their direction.

"Get down," Finn yelled, one arm swinging out to force her head toward her knees.

Rapid gunfire ripped across the truck in the next heartbeat, shattering the windshield and raining a storm of pebbled glass over her back as she screamed.

Chapter Seventeen

A few phone calls later, Finn walked the crime scene with Dean, a pair of officers and a detective from his team. His pickup would be towed to a local shop for repair after the bullet casings were located. Dean and Austin had come to the rescue with a company-owned SUV. Dean would ride back with Austin. Hayley and Finn would keep the vehicle owned by the PI firm as long as they needed.

Meanwhile, Hayley sat in Austin's pickup, watching safely from a short distance. Austin, for his part, played the role of shocked citizen, gaping at the chaos, only there to comfort a shaken friend. He would see everything from his vantage point that Finn and those walking the crime scene would miss.

"What do you think?" Dean asked, folding his arms and turning his attention to Finn. "Everett followed you down the drive because he had some place to be. Was the shooting about you and Hayley or him?"

Finn rubbed his stubbled chin and scanned the broader area. His gaze slid over the squat navy blue convertible still parked behind his truck. The car's owner rocked from foot to foot several feet away, speaking with officers again. He'd made multiple phone calls, likely to his lawyers, and retreated into his home twice, but he kept boomeranging back. "Any idea where he was headed?"

"He had a reservation at the country club's restaurant," Dean said.

"Standing day and time?" Finn asked.

If Mr. Everett was a creature of habit, and someone wanted him dead, knowing when and where to expect him would make the work easy. It was the main reason Finn continuously warned women in self-defense classes not to create obvious routines in their daily lives. They never knew who was watching, or what motive they might have. For a determined killer, catching Everett leaving his driveway on a low-traffic residential road was far better than at the busy club.

Still, Everett had been in the hot tub when they'd arrived.

"Nope." Dean arched an eyebrow. "This reservation was set today."

"Who called it in?"

Dean shrugged. "My contact at the club didn't say. Only that the reservation wasn't on the books when she got there this morning."

Finn grunted. It was possible whoever wanted Everett dead had a contact at the club who'd tipped them off about his new reservation. Or maybe they'd simply been waiting outside the home for him to leave. Thankfully, Austin was keeping watch now. He would know if anyone on the street seemed suspicious and contact Finn as soon as he spotted them.

A rookie officer Finn recognized as Traci Landers moved in his direction, and the brothers parted slightly to make room for her in the small huddle.

"Learn anything good?" Finn asked, flicking his gaze in Mr. Everett's direction.

Officer Landers followed his attention, then turned back with a nod. "He thinks whoever killed his wife is targeting him now, and he's requested a patrol for his safety."

"I like that," Finn said. "Let's get him a babysitter. I want him safe if he's in danger, and if this is all some sort of ruse, I want to know that too. Get someone good to watch him. Someone who'll pick up on anything that doesn't seem right."

"Will do," Landers said. "We've collected several casings from the shots fired. I'm taking those to the lab. If the same weapon has been used in any other crimes on record, we'll know soon."

More importantly, they'd know whether or not these bullets matched the one the coroner pulled from Kate.

Officer Landers's brow furrowed as she looked more closely at Finn. "You sure you don't want the medic to take a look at you?"

He forced his eyes to meet hers, determined not to look at the new cuts on his arms and cheek. Pebbles of broken windshield had nicked his skin, drawing fresh blood and staining his truck seat. "Nothing a little alcohol and peroxide won't heal." The windshield would be easy to replace. Bloodstained leather was another story. One he didn't want to think about. At least the cuts would take care of themselves.

Thankfully, Hayley had been physically unscathed. Emotionally, she'd been stunned silent, possibly in shock, though she'd also refused the medic.

Officer Landers tipped a finger to her hat and stepped away.

"How's Hayley holding up?" Dean asked, gaze drifting to Austin's truck. "I imagine social work isn't usually so brutal."

Finn gripped the back of his neck, hating that she'd been through any of the dangerous and heartbreaking things she'd experienced lately. "She's tougher than she looks." And he'd only recently learned the whole truth of that statement. Hayley had faced obstacles and had the odds stacked against her all her life. Yet here she was, a heart larger and warmer than the sun, proving that children weren't doomed to repeat the flawed lives of their parents and that sometimes those who'd had it the hardest learned to love the biggest.

Finn began to move in her direction before he'd made the conscious decision to do so. Hayley needed a safe place to recuperate, rest and heal. He wanted to be that for her. "I'm heading out," he told Dean. "Keep me posted."

"Where are you going?"

"I'm taking Hayley home."

No words had ever felt sweeter.

HAYLEY STOOD IN Finn's small bathroom, thankful for an incredible distraction from the sheer chaos of the last several days. Outside those walls, nothing seemed to be going her way. Inside, however, she couldn't complain.

Finn leaned against the counter, patiently allowing her to clean and rebandage a few of his deeper wounds. Some of the injuries he'd received during the explosion were out of his reach and in need of care following his shower. Hayley didn't need to be asked twice.

She swabbed each cut and puncture with an alcohol pad, then dabbed a fresh layer of ointment onto the angry, reddened skin before applying a new patch of gauze and medical tape. She tried not to steal unnecessary glances at his handsome face and bare chest in the still steamy bathroom mirror. And she refused the barrage of clear memories, reminding her of all the ways she'd touched and been touched by Finn Beaumont.

He winced slightly as she covered the worst of his cuts, and she paused before continuing her work. The kisses they'd recently shared, and the sweet words they'd exchanged, had meant a lot. But when the strongest man she knew humbled himself to ask for her help with something so personal, she knew she'd regained his trust. Trust was everything. And his willingness to be vulnerable spoke volumes.

Finn's strength and perseverance benefited everyone, but those same traits came at a price for him. Especially when accepting help with the little things. She'd seen him help his family build a pole barn in a week, but refused to get help tying his shoes after fracturing his wrist taking down a drunk-and-disorderly.

Her heart fluttered as their eyes met in the mirror's reflection. She set aside the tape. "Finished."

He swept his shirt off the countertop and threaded it over his head. "I appreciate it."

"Anytime. I appreciate all the things you do for me too."

Finn turned to face her, a smile playing on his lips. "I suppose I have to make you dinner?"

Hayley scoffed, eagerly playing along. "Of course, you do. Don't make me call your mama."

"Don't even joke about that." His strong arms snaked out, gripping her waist and moving her close on a laugh.

She arched as goose bumps scattered over her skin. The thrill of possibility burst in her chest. Finn's guard was down. He'd left the serious parts of himself somewhere else in favor of this precious, carefree moment with her.

She melted against him, hanging on with delight.

He buried his face against her neck, holding her as if she was his life preserver and not the other way around. "I am so sorry you were in that truck with me today," he whispered. "Or at that warehouse. All I ever want to do is protect you, and I'm failing miserably."

"You're not."

Heat from his nearness, his tone, the scent of him was all around her, igniting fire in her veins. She moaned as his lips drew a path along the rim of her ear. "Finn?" she asked, sliding her hands beneath the hem of his shirt.

He pulled back, blinking unfocused eyes, visibly struggling for control. "Too much?" he rasped.

"More."

Strong fingers burrowed into her hair, cradling her head. Then his mouth took hers in a deep, tantalizing kiss.

She traced the ridges of his abs and planes of his broad chest with greedy fingers, pushing the fabric of his shirt upward, exposing miles of tanned skin.

Finn broke the kiss, eyes wild and searching. His lips tipped into a wolfish grin at whatever he saw in her expression. Then he reached over his head and freed the shirt he'd just put on.

Emboldened, she did the same. Her shirt landed in a discarded puddle beside his, earning a low, toe-curling growl from Finn.

She tipped her chin in challenge and ran a fingertip down his torso to the waistband of his pants.

Another cuss crossed his lips, followed by a cautious plea. "Are you sure?"

She rose onto her toes, pressing her body against his warm skin. "Take me to bed, Detective."

Finn didn't need to be asked twice.

He gripped her hips in his hands and hauled her off the ground in one burst of movement.

A delighted squeal erupted from her chest as he swept her off her feet, and strode easily to his room.

She pulled him down with her, onto his sheets, and enjoyed the view.

He held himself above her, palms planted beside each

of her shoulders, elbows locked. An expression of awe and admiration graced his handsome face. "I've missed you," he said softly. "So damn much."

"I've missed you too." She rose to meet him, kissing him slowly and drawing him down to her. She savored each mind-bending sweep of his tongue and expert stroke of his hand, feeling more beautiful and cherished than she had in far too long. Since the last time she'd been with him.

When there was nothing more between them, and their bodies rocked together to a perfect end, there was no denying her love for Finn Beaumont. As strong and resilient as the man himself.

She could only hope he might feel the same way again one day.

FINN SLIPPED AWAY from Hayley when her breaths grew long and even, her body taken by sleep. They'd talked for hours, clinging to one another and making up for a year of lost time. But when Hayley had drifted off, Finn's mind had begun to race.

Moonlight streamed through the window onto her beautifully peaceful face, and he kissed her cheek before he rose. His heart broke anew at the thought of losing her again. He probably should've taken things more slowly, not been so greedy. Shouldn't have risked scaring her away. But her sweet kisses and tender urging had reduced his logic to rubble. And he'd taken her at her word. She wanted him. He needed her. Shamelessly, he regretted nothing.

He only hoped she'd feel the same in the morning.

Finn tugged on his T-shirt and sweatpants, then padded into the living room, grabbing a bottle of water and his laptop from the kitchen on his way. He had files and transcripts to review. Lab reports and evidence photos to request. Maybe he'd even find a lead they could follow in the morning. Something that would bring them closer to locating Gage and Parker, or Kate's killer.

He took a seat on the couch and booted up his laptop, then waited for his usual browser windows to load. He logged in to his work email, forcing images of a climaxing Hayley from his mind.

He had a lot of work to do if he wanted to gain her love and trust again.

He'd have to be careful not to scare her away. He'd take his time and watch her for signs she was ready, because he couldn't lose her again.

The computer on his lap brought him back to the moment, to the awful reminder that he and Hayley had shared one too many near-death experiences this week. Until he found the culprit, it was only a matter of time before there was another drive-by shooting or explosion. And he needed to locate Gage and Parker before the killer found them instead.

Finn's inbox was full, as always, so he started at the top.

Several hours later, he'd worked through every message, reviewed every shared document, interview transcript and piece of evidence from crimes related to Kate's death. He'd replayed news footage and listened to audio files from interrogations until his heavy, scratchy eyes drifted shut.

He woke to the sound of his ringing phone and peeled his eyes open to blazing sunlight through the front window. His laptop rested on the floor beside the couch, where he'd accidentally fallen asleep.

Finn swiveled upright, planting his feet on the floor and searching the space around him for his phone. "Beaumont," he answered, catching the call before it went to voice mail.

"Are you sleeping?" Dean asked, his voice a tone of mock horror. "It's after seven."

Finn rubbed a hand over his tired eyes and mussed hair. "I had a late night."

"Oh, yeah?" His brother's tone implied the reason had been Hayley.

Finn supposed his brother was right on a number of counts.

A fresh bolt of panic lanced his gut. "Oh, no." He'd left her in bed so he could slip away and work. If she'd woken without him during the night, she was sure to think— "Hey, can I call you back," Finn asked abruptly, already moving toward the hallway. "Unless you've got news. Then let me have it, and I'll call you back after that."

"No," Dean said. "I was just calling to say Mama's on her way to your place with breakfast, and I'm hungry, so I'm coming too. I figured we can talk shop over cheesy grits and hash browns."

Finn spun back to face the front window. "How long ago did she leave?"

"I'm not sure. She was gone when I got there," Dean said. "Dad pointed me in your direction. Honestly, if I knew I'd have to drive all over town for my breakfast, I could've picked something up on my way to work."

"It's not too late for that," Finn said.

"I don't know," Dean said. "I'm committed to those grits."

"See you when you get here." Finn disconnected outside his partially closed bedroom door. "Hayley?" He rapped his knuckles gently on the frame. "Are you up?"

"Yeah."

Finn stepped cautiously into the room.

She sat on the edge of the bed, dressed in cut-off jean shorts and a faded blue T-shirt. She'd pulled her thick hair away from her face in a ponytail. Her expression was guarded and wary.

"Mom and Dean are on their ways over for breakfast." He smiled. "You sleep well?"

Hayley nodded and stood, her phone clutched in one hand.

"News?" he asked, looking pointedly at the little device, and hoping she planned to speak soon. He couldn't have ruined things for them already. Could he?

"Nothing yet," she said. "I was hoping, but—"

"Hey." Finn extended an arm as she approached, then wrapped it around her when she tried to pass him. "Can I make you some coffee while we wait for Mama?"

"That sounds nice. Thank you."

Finn sighed and let his head fall forward, tightening his grip a bit when she tried to get away. He raised his eyes to hers and waited for Hayley to meet his gaze. "I snuck away to work last night. I was trying to find a thread to pull on this case. I didn't mean to fall asleep out there. I was supposed to get back here after I finished reviewing files."

Her cheeks darkened, and she averted her gaze. "It's okay. I get it."

Finn raised his hands to cup her cheeks. "I mean it. I wanted to be right here with you."

She looked into his eyes, scanning, seeking.

The doorbell rang.

He held his ground for another long beat then pressed a tender kiss to her forehead before relenting. "Come on." He slid his hand over hers. "We'd better let Mama in before she jimmies the lock."

Hayley laughed softly, and a measure of weight rolled off his shoulders. "She wouldn't."

"Probably not," he admitted. "But she's fully capable, and I don't want to test her."

He led Hayley down the hall, and she broke away at the kitchen. He turned toward the front door. "Morning, Mama," he said, inviting her in a moment later with a hug.

"Morning, sweet boy." She patted his cheek and passed him a set of thermal casserole bags. "Breakfast is in there. Where's Hayley?"

"I'm here," Hayley called. "Making coffee. Would you like a cup?"

"Oh, yes, please!"

His brother's truck appeared at the end of Finn's driveway, so he left the door open and headed for the kitchen. "Dean just pulled up."

Finn unpacked his mom's casseroles while she pulled dishes from the cupboards and silverware from the drawer.

"Knock, knock," Dean said, stepping inside and closing the door behind him. "Something smells great." He greeted his mother and Hayley with hugs, then offered raised eyebrows to Finn. "You look beat."

"Sit," their mom ordered. "Let's talk over breakfast."

The meal became a business meeting, as expected, and Finn kept one hand on Hayley as often as possible.

She blushed and hid behind her mug when his mother looked in their direction a little too long, but she didn't make any effort to push him away. A good sign, he hoped.

"And now we're waiting for something else to come up," Dean said, concluding a lengthy list of places he and Austin had looked for Gage and Parker during the night.

"Do you have any other ideas?" his mother asked Hayley.

"No, ma'am. I wish I did."

Finn gathered her empty plate and cup, then pressed a kiss to her temple as he stood. "Can I get you anything else?"

His mother's eyes bulged and a smile wider than the Atlantic spread over her pink cheeks.

Dean shook his head.

"Well, I'm not worried," Finn said, setting their plates into the sink. The words were true enough, even if he wasn't sure what to do next. "Things always seem the worst right before a big break."

They still needed to visit the country club. See if anyone thought Mr. Everett and Mr. Forester were closer than they claimed. Or if there was anything else another member might want to share.

"True," Dean agreed, taking another swig from his mug. "It's some kind of phenomenon. Just when things start to look impossible in a case, they take off full-speed."

Hayley didn't look swayed. "What about all the cold cases out there?"

Dean frowned.

Finn tried not to smile. She had a point, but this case wasn't destined to go unfinished. Not if he could help it.

"Okay." She released an audible sigh. "Did anyone find out if Kate had a prenup? Her husband seemed squirrelly, and he had a lot to gain from her death."

"My team has confirmed the prenup," Finn said. "But not the specifics. According to a memo I read last night, they've put in a request with the Everett family lawyer and a local judge, hoping one of the two will comply. They've requested financial records as well."

Finn's phone vibrated, and he shifted to pull the device from his pocket. The name on the screen sent his attention to Hayley. "It's Eric."

She straightened. "The middle school's groundskeeper?"

"Yeah."

The room fell silent as he accepted the call using the speaker option. "Beaumont."

"Hey, kid, this might be a long shot," the older man said,

bypassing a traditional greeting. "But Gage Myers has been on my mind since the moment you told me what's going on with him. And I recalled his father being an incredible artist."

That tracked, given the talent Gage had shown in his street art. "Go on," Finn said.

"Like I said, this might be nothing, but I remember the two of them spending a lot of time at a little art studio on the bay. His father used to lead classes there for students at the middle school. I'm not sure the place is used much anymore. He was the main volunteer, and the program was funded by an arts project that he organized."

Hayley covered her mouth, eyes springing wide.

And just like that, they had a new lead.

Chapter Eighteen

The art studio Eric had mentioned was a small rectangular building overlooking the bay. The clapboard structure was schoolhouse-red and perched upon tall wooden pillars that had been darkened and worn from weather and age. An abundance of windows faced the water, and a broad wooden deck stretched into the gravel parking lot out back.

A dense thicket of leafy trees cast heavy shade over the structure, effectively hiding it from the road. Hayley walked toward the deck stairs slowly, immediately thankful for a break from the sweltering sun. Multicolored handprints adorned the glass beside floating images of paint palettes, brushes and smocks. Wooden easels had been permanently anchored to the railing, securing them from storms and assuring they'd be there for any artist in need. Sunny yellow letters stenciled on a blue door encouraged guests to enter.

She climbed the steps and tried the knob, but it didn't turn. "Locked," she said, searching over her shoulder for Finn, who'd disappeared.

She moved to the window, scanning for signs of movement, then cupped her hands around her eyes to peer inside. A shadow outside a window on the opposite side of the quiet building peered back.

Finn's familiar face became clear, as clouds passed over the sun. He pointed to something in the space between them.

Hayley adjusted her hands and gaze to find a long table covered in a blanket, the tip of a pillow poking out on the floor beneath. She straightened and hurried to the door, then knocked. "Gage? Parker? It's me, Hayley. Are you in there?"

Her heart jolted and hammered at the possibility she'd finally found the boys. They were safe, and they'd been well hidden in the old art studio. Protected from the sun and weather. They might've had access to running water and they'd had at least one blanket and pillow. It was more than she'd dared to hope. Images of the kids huddled together in a filthy, crumbling structure in Old Downtown had haunted her dreams. "Gage? Are you okay? I've been so worried. Please answer."

The wooden stairs behind her creaked, and she spun on a sharp intake of breath.

Finn stilled, palms up. "It's just me."

She pressed a hand to her chest and rushed back to the window for another look. "The boys made that blanket fort. Right?"

"I'm hoping," Finn said.

She tried opening the window, but it was secure. "How did they get in?"

"I don't know. The windows on the other side are all locked too." Finn gave the old blue door a thorough inspection, then dragged his fingers along the wooden trim overhead.

"Maybe Gage knew where to find a key," she suggested, recognizing Finn's attempt to do the same.

"Maybe, but I don't," Finn said, extracting a credit card from his wallet. "So it looks like I have to break in."

She returned to him with a smile. "I hoped you'd say that."

He slid the plastic rectangle between the door and frame,

then wiggled the knob while he worked the card. A moment later, the door opened.

"You're actual magic," Hayley said, slipping inside while he put away the credit card.

"More like a reformed troublemaker, but I like your take a little better."

She flipped the light switch beside the door. Nothing happened. "I guess no one paid the bill lately."

"Judging by the layer of dust on the windows and countertops, I'd say it's been a while since the place was used as more than a hideout," Finn said.

The wide wooden floorboards were splattered with a rainbow of spilled paints. The walls were covered in murals of the sand and sea. Forgotten art projects hung from the hand drawn waves and surf. A countertop with a sink overlooked the rear deck. The rest of the building was an uninterrupted space, save for a room with an open door on their right.

Finn tapped his phone to life, and a moment later a beam of light illuminated the area. He headed toward the door.

Hayley wiped sweat from her forehead as she crouched to peek under the table covered by a blanket. Candy and snack wrappers littered the area inside the tiny fort. A second blanket covered the floor and empty water bottles had been flattened in the corner. A small notebook kept a tally of food and drinks, along with prices. On pages further back, a hangman game was in progress. Two words, four letters for the first, five for the second. The phrase *don't worry*, minus the two *o's*, had been revealed.

Her heart ached as she clutched the notebook to her chest and stood. "They were here," she said. "This is Gage's handwriting."

Finn returned to her, extinguishing the light. "There's

a supply closet and restroom back there. The shelves are mostly bare. What's that?"

Hayley passed the book to him.

He examined the pages before returning the item to her. Then he squatted for a look at the space beneath the table. "Was he budgeting?"

"Looks like it. Should we wait for them to come back?" she asked, hoping the answer was yes.

Finn stretched to his full height. "I'll ask Dean to keep watch from afar. They might avoid returning if they see anyone nearby. You're probably right about Gage knowing where to find a spare key to this place since his dad spent so much time here. He's smart. I don't know who'd think to look for him at this place."

"Where do you think they got the snacks and water?" Hayley said.

Finn anchored his hands on his hips and shook his head. "I don't know."

"We should visit the closest convenience stores. See if anyone remembers them."

"That sounds like a plan," Finn said. He opened his arm in the direction of the door they'd used to enter. "After you."

Hayley bent to return the notebook, but as she placed it under the table, a new idea came to mind. "Can I leave a note for the boys?"

Finn smiled. "Absolutely. Make sure they have all our contact information. My folks' and brothers' numbers too."

She retrieved a pencil from atop the blanket, then began to write. She didn't stop until she was satisfied Gage understood the danger he was in and all the people who were on his side.

She sent up prayers for the boys' protection as she left the little studio, then climbed back into the borrowed SUV.

Finn navigated the scenic byway, the sound on one side, miles of marsh and natural sand dunes on the other. His attention bounced routinely from road to rearview mirror, likely watching for a tail.

Hayley kept her eyes glued to the coastline in search of a small shop or café. People were creatures of habit. If she and Finn found the place where the boys had gotten their snacks and water, they'd probably know where to expect them to shop again.

Less than a mile later, a small orange building appeared. The building's paint was faded and blistered by unhindered sunlight. An attached dock extending into the water was lined in stacks of brightly colored kayaks and paddleboards. The sign at the roadside declared the business to be Eco Exploration, Marshal's Bluff's premier nature-excursion-and-tour company.

"We have a tour company?" Hayley asked.

The SUV slowed.

"Three, believe it or not," Finn said, engaging the turn signal. "The others target fishermen and head out to sea. This place does dolphin-sighting boat tours and gets folks onto the water for exploring and appreciating the natural beauty here."

"Huh." She unbuckled when he parked, then joined him in the lot. "I forget to soak in the views sometimes. I need to make a point of it when this ends."

Finn slid mischievous eyes her way. "You still kayak?"

"Not as much as I should." She'd hidden behind her work since their breakup. But she was healing now, and all the near-death experiences were heavy reminders that she'd only live once. Her job helped a lot of people, but she needed to make time for herself. Take weekends and evenings to recuperate and soak up the beauty around her. "Any chance they sell snacks and water?" she asked.

"About one hundred percent." Finn stopped at the open shop door and motioned her inside ahead of him.

She crossed the threshold and plucked the fabric of her shirt away from her chest.

Box fans rattled in the open windows, and a pitiful cross breeze from one open door to the other stirred a dusting of sand on the floor.

"No tours today," a young woman at the counter called. Her cheeks were ruddy from the heat, and she fanned her face with a clipboard. "Storm's coming."

Hayley envied the woman's string-bikini top and cutoff shorts, but doubted they were small enough to prevent her inevitable heatstroke if she stayed inside much longer. "We don't need a tour," she said as kindly as possible. "I'm a social worker looking for two missing children. We thought you might've seen them."

The woman's expression turned from bored to alarmed. "Do you have a picture?"

"Of the older boy," Hayley said. She flipped through the images on her phone in search of a recent shot of Gage.

"Have you seen a lot of children this week?" Finn asked, pulling the woman's attention to him.

Her lips parted, and she blinked.

Hayley fought a smile. The Beaumont men had that effect on women. The best part was that none of them seemed to know.

"Yes," she answered belatedly. "It's our busy season. Tourists," she added.

"The boys we're looking for are eight and fourteen," Hayley said. "They're in danger, and it's imperative that we find them before they're harmed." She found a selfie of Gage with a surfboard and turned the phone to face the woman. "They might've bought some drinks and snacks."

Hayley had taken Gage to the beach once, because he said that was where he felt most at peace, and it was his first summer without his parents to take him.

The woman's eyebrows rose and she levered herself off her stool. "I've seen them," she said excitedly. "They didn't buy anything, but they were in here yesterday hanging around when a tour was about to leave. I asked where their mom was, and the older one said she was already on the boat. So I told them to hurry up or they'd miss it, and they left."

A spike of hope and joy shot through Hayley. Gage and Parker had been in the same store where she was standing, only a day before. And they'd been okay. She turned to look for Finn.

He tipped his head in the direction of a wire display stand near the open door to the dock. The same snacks she'd seen in the blanket fort were represented. A small refrigeration unit hummed beside the rack. Bottles of water were visible beyond the glass door.

This was where the boys had gotten their foodstuffs.

She smiled as she realized the list of snacks and prices Gage had made wasn't a result of him managing a budget. He'd tracked the things he'd taken to survive. As if he might've planned to pay later.

"Thank you," Hayley said, turning back to the woman. "If you see them again, will you call me?" She extracted a business card from her bag and passed it to the woman. "Actually. Will you give them a note?"

The woman nodded, expression soft. "Of course."

Hayley wrote a similar letter to the one she'd left at the studio, then passed it to the clerk. "I appreciate this so much. And I'd like a bottle of water." She handed the woman enough money to cover the drink and the boys' snacks. "Keep the change."

She smiled brightly at Hayley. "I'm glad to help."

Outside, the breeze had picked up, and Hayley inhaled deeply, glad to be free of the stuffy building. Beads of sweat formed on her upper lip and brow as they moved toward their ride. The boys would need water soon. "We should wait here and see if they come back."

"I still want to visit the country club," Finn said, unlocking the SUV so they could climb inside. He started the engine and pumped up the air-conditioning, apparently not as impervious to the heat as he seemed.

Hayley wet her lips, anxiety rising in her chest at the thought of leaving this place. "We know the boys have been here and the art studio. I think we should split up and keep watch over both."

Finn frowned. "We're not splitting up. You've been in just as much danger as they have. More, as far as I know. So you're staying with me. Dean will stake out the studio."

"Finn—" Her protest was cut short by the ringing of his phone.

He raised a finger, letting her know he needed to take the call. Then he raised the device to his ear. "Beaumont."

Hayley scanned the nearby road, trees and parking lot while she waited, willing the boys to appear. She was so close to finding them. Practically walking in their footsteps. Separated only by a day.

"When?" Finn asked, pulling her eyes back to him. He shifted the SUV into gear and pressed the phone between his ear and shoulder as he drew the safety belt across his torso. "I'm on my way." He disconnected the call and dropped the phone into the cupholder. A heartbeat later, the SUV tore away from the shack with a spray of dust and gravel.

Hayley grabbed her seat belt, snapping it into place as the tires hit asphalt and they rocketed forward. "What happened?"

"Police Chief Harmen called a press conference. The team got a hit on the SUV from the drive-by. A doorbell camera belonging to one of Everett's neighbors recorded the shooting, and Tech Services pulled a partial license-plate number. It's the same SUV that was seen near the explosion and caught on the news near Kate's death site. The vehicle is registered to Lance Stevens. He's being picked up and hauled in for questioning."

Chapter Nineteen

Finn ignored the speed limit on the way back to town. The scenic byway they traveled was meant to be taken slowly and enjoyed, but there wasn't anything he'd enjoy more today than meeting Lance Stevens. The name of the man being brought in for questioning, possibly the one responsible for repeatedly putting Hayley in danger, circled in his mind. Had the man worked alone? Or was this crime spree his own? And if so, why?

Finn would've requested to perform the interview himself if he thought he was the better choice for the job. Unfortunately, he wasn't convinced he'd stop himself from flattening the suspect given an opportunity. And he couldn't afford to damage any chance they had at building a case that would put Mr. Stevens away for a very long time.

News of today's press conference was nearly as intriguing as news of a suspect. Finn could only assume one was directly related to the other. Police Chief Harmen wasn't one to waste time unnecessarily, or interact with the media when he could avoid it. Given the widespread interest in Katherine Everett's death, he expected everyone in town would be tuned in, and anyone with a camera and microphone would be outside the precinct, hoping for a front-row seat.

Unfortunately for Finn, he and Hayley had been as far from the police station as possible without leaving Marshal's Bluff, and the return trip was infuriatingly long.

Traffic thickened as he reached the blocks nearest the station, slowing their progress further. News trucks clogged the streets and reporters hurried on foot toward the squat brick building in question. A row of cruisers stood guard inside the gate, looking authoritative and giving the impression of protection. The display of a formidable team. From the number of squad cars alone, he knew there were enough hands on deck to keep the conference orderly and peaceful.

"This is a lot of people," Hayley said, giving voice to his thought. "It's nice that so many folks care about what he wants to say, but I've never been a fan of crowds."

Finn completely understood. People were fine. People were smart. Crowds were often chaotic, thoughtless and emotional. A dangerous combination.

The station doors opened as Finn crept along behind a caravan of gawkers and rubberneckers. The chief of police strode onto the concrete steps and into view.

Hayley tuned the SUV's radio to the call numbers of a station represented by a nearby news van.

A female announcer's voice broke through the speakers. "…here for you live from the Marshal's Bluff police station, where Chief Harmen has called a press conference on the case of Katherine Everett."

Finn grimaced. He could only imagine what the details on his case would sound like through the filtered lens of local media. After everything he and Hayley had been through this week, he wanted the information firsthand. "Hang on," he said, turning his eyes back to the road. He pressed the gas pedal and turned the wheel, causing cars to honk and onlookers to complain.

"What are you doing?" Hayley asked, pressing a palm against the dashboard to steady herself as he angled the vehicle onto the curb outside the station's open gate.

"Getting us a parking space." He unlocked the doors and climbed out, then waited for Hayley to join him. Dark clouds raced overhead as he took her hand and towed her past a set of uniformed officers.

Finn wasn't usually a superstitious man, but the sudden shadow cast upon this moment felt like a bad omen. He pulled Hayley closer in response. He flashed his detective's shield as he pushed his way to the front of the crowd, where an array of microphones on stands had been arranged.

Chief Harmen's eyes caught Finn's, and he gave a small shake of his head.

Finn straightened. Something had gone wrong.

"Hello," the chief said, effectively quieting the crowd. "I'm Police Chief Harmen, and this press conference has been called to update you on the investigation into Katherine Everett's murder. A male suspect has been identified in connection to that crime and several other crimes we believe to be related. We do not yet know if the suspect worked alone or in conjunction with others. Additionally, we are not releasing the name of the suspect at this time. However, you can be assured that despite his attorney's best attempts, we will not be swayed from finishing the work we've started. Katherine Everett, her family, friends and the community, will see justice served."

Frustration tightened Finn's muscles. He wouldn't be able to listen in on the interview of Lance Stevens today. Not because traffic had made him late, but because the criminal's attorney had likely already escorted him home. Either Stevens had money, or someone who did had interceded on his behalf. Kate's husband and Conrad Forester came instantly to mind.

"The investigation remains fluid and active at this time," Chief Harmen continued. "Anyone with information about the death of Katherine Everett, the warehouse explosion in Old Downtown or the recent shooting outside the Everett family estate should contact Marshal's Bluff PD. Thank you. Now, I'll take a few questions."

The crowd erupted in shouts, every member of the media vying to be heard and chosen.

Finn pressed the pads of his fingers to his closed eyelids.

"Hey." Hayley tugged his hands away from his face, meeting his tired eyes with her sincere gaze. "It's just a setback. Things always start moving fast when they seem to be at a standstill, right?"

His lips twitched, fighting a small smile as she returned the words of their earlier conversation to him. "I believe I've heard that somewhere."

Hayley held on to his hands as he let them drop. "I can't believe Stevens's attorney got here before we did," she said. "Summoning a public defender when I need one for a case can take forever."

He gave her fingers a gentle squeeze. "Money can't buy peace or happiness, but it can keep a lawyer on retainer."

Hayley frowned. "Who do you suppose paid for this one?"

"An excellent question." If the lawyer wasn't Stevens's, then whoever sent him over here likely had good reason. And that information would be priceless.

"Please!" Chief Harmen hollered into the mics, pumping his palms up and down in a failed attempt to regain control. "I'd appreciate your patience while I try to hear from a few more members of the media."

The rev of a motorcycle drew Finn's attention to the slow-moving traffic outside the gate. A driver in black leather with a matching helmet and mirrored visor slowed his ride to a crawl and set his feet on the ground to steady himself.

"Chief Harmen," a female voice called loudly, "can you comment on rumors that a fourteen-year-old boy is suspected in the shooting and bludgeoning death of Katherine Everett? Or that he is now considered a fugitive on the run?"

Hayley gasped, and Finn spun to face the crowd, attempting to identify the woman who'd spoken.

He needed to find that reporter and ask where she'd gotten that information. Someone had clearly fed her the lies to generate another narrative, or worse, to put the entire community on the lookout for Gage.

Sudden rapid gunfire blasted through the air, and Hayley dropped to the ground, pulling Finn down with her.

Screams and chaos erupted as he checked her for injuries.

"I'm okay," she said. "But they aren't."

He followed her trembling finger to several fallen crowd members. Honking horns and the sounds of multiple fender benders formed the backdrop to barking tires and the growl of a motorcycle engine.

The driver angled away, guiding his ride between stopped cars, seeking a path for escape.

"Stay here," Finn demanded, pushing Hayley toward the police station's steps. "Go inside. Tell them who you are and that I went after the shooter. He's on a black motorcycle stuck in traffic. Don't leave!" He freed his weapon and made a run for the waiting SUV.

The motorcycle jumped onto the sidewalk and rounded the corner, now out of sight.

Finn dove into his vehicle and gunned the engine to life.

He squeezed the SUV between parked cars and a nearby shop, knocking off his passenger mirror in the process. On the next block, he had the motorcycle in his sights, and he lifted his cell phone to call for backup.

HAYLEY STARED AFTER FINN, stunned motionless as he climbed into the SUV and raced away.

Around her, people panicked, screaming and running around mindlessly. Some toward the building. Some into the street. Others rushed to help the injured, who were lying in puddles of blood on the ground.

Several uniformed officers climbed into waiting cruisers, eager to give chase, just as Finn had. Except the cruisers were blocked by traffic and throngs of frightened citizens.

In the distance, ambulance sirens wailed to life.

Hayley shoved herself upright, struggling to process the horror. An armed gunman was on the loose, and Finn had gone after him. The realization of what might happen next gripped her chest and squeezed. Her breaths were short, and her head lightened uncomfortably. What if the next person to take a bullet was Finn? Who would help him?

A set of strong hands curled over her biceps and turned her in a new direction. "Let's get you out of here."

Hayley pulled back, intuition flaring. "No. I'm okay, thank y—" Words froze on her tongue as she took in the man at her side.

Conrad Forester, the CEO of Lighthouse, Inc., glared back, and his grip on her tightened. He appeared presentable and calm in a sharp gray suit and red tie, as if he'd only been present for the press conference like everyone else. "Let me rephrase. Come with me now, and do not cause any trouble, or those boys will die."

Finn kept the motorcycle in view as he radioed for backup. Dispatch assigned two cars, but neither were close, and the cruisers from the precinct were several minutes behind. The motorcycle zigzagged through traffic, keeping a steady pace and changing directions frequently, trying and failing to shake Finn.

The vehicle darted into the shadows of an overpass, and Finn plunged in behind.

He blinked, adjusting his eyes to the darkness a moment before readjusting them to the sun on the other side. "He's getting on the highway near Mill Street," Finn called, projecting his voice toward the phone in the cupholder, Dispatch on the other end of the line.

A dozen similar motorcycles appeared in the space of his next heartbeat, all joining the first and forming a pack. Instinct raised the hairs on his arms, and suddenly he wasn't so sure he'd been a top-tier tail and not a detective engaged in a trap.

He pressed the gas pedal to the floor, determined to keep his eye on the motorcycle carrying the shooter, but the bikes began to weave in and out of lanes. An 85-mile-per-hour game of cups.

Then the central interchange appeared. A mass of twinning highways with multiple on- and off-ramps made it impossible to know which lane to stay in. Increasing traffic made it harder to maneuver quickly. But the pack of motorcycles split up, scattering in every direction, and Finn realized the whole truth. It didn't matter which lane he was in, because he couldn't follow them all.

He'd been tricked.

Chapter Twenty

Mr. Forester led Hayley through the chaos of a terrorized crowd to a waiting sedan. Her limbs felt numb, and all hope of rescue vanished as his threat settled into her heart and mind. He had Gage and Parker. And he'd hurt them if she drew attention to herself or tried to run away.

"Get in," he whispered. The words landed harshly against her hair. The heat and scent of his sour breath knotted her stomach, and she rolled her shoulders forward, wishing she could curl into a ball or hide.

She dropped onto the passenger seat as instructed, then flinched at the slamming of the door beside her. Outside the tinted glass, uniformed officers rushed to calm the crowd. They looked everywhere except in her direction, too distracted by the recent shots fired and a line of incoming ambulances.

Traffic moved, making room for the emergency vehicles to pass.

Forester shifted into Drive and took advantage of the cleared road, making a casual getaway.

She wiped silent tears from her cheeks as they left her only means of rescue behind. "Where are you taking me?" she asked.

Quaint shops and clueless pedestrians passed on historic sidewalks beyond her window.

"Somewhere you can't ruin my life." He stole a look in her direction, head shaking in disgust. "All because some punk kid saw something he shouldn't have, and you couldn't let it go."

"Gage is a good kid," Hayley snapped. "He's alone and scared in this world, and he saw you kill a woman. Of course, he ran. What was he supposed to do?"

"He was supposed to mind his own damn business. And so were you!"

Hayley jumped at his sudden yell, the malice in his tone turning her blood to ice. Any chance she'd hoped to have at reasoning with her abductor was gone. He was clearly on a mission to silence her and nothing more.

He didn't even seem guilty or ashamed. Only outraged that he'd been caught committing murder.

"Why'd you do it?" she asked. *If I'm going to die*, she reasoned, *I might as well understand why.* "Why kill Kate? Was it because her plans for a homeless shelter and community center interfered with your plans to build parks and condos? Did you even consider trying to compromise before you bludgeoned and shot her?"

He pulled his attention from the road to stare at her for a long beat, eyes hard, expression feral. "She would've cost me tens of millions with that roach trap. People don't want to raise their kids beside a homeless shelter, or walk their little doodle dogs past park benches with junkies passed out on them. I tried to buy her out. I'm not the bad guy here. She refused to take my offer, and it was well over what she'd paid for her properties. She had something against other people getting rich. As if she was the only one in this town who deserved nice things. She was a greedy, selfish—"

Suddenly the sirens that had been small in the distance grew insistent and loud, interrupting Forester's tirade and pulling his attention to the rearview mirror. "Besides, this isn't all on me. Topper owes me. I couldn't reason with her, so he was supposed to."

Hayley twisted in her seat, craning for a look at the police cruisers racing into view behind them. Cars and trucks slowed and moved out of their way.

She dared a breath of hope.

Forester hit his turn signal and took the next right toward Old Downtown. The cruisers raced past, continuing toward the highway.

Forrester chuckled. "Those aren't for us. No need to worry."

She swallowed a lump of bile, worried again for Finn.

"I'm guessing your detective had a little trouble catching my friend," Forester said. "There's no shame in that. My friend is very good," he clarified. "Not your detective. If he was any good, you wouldn't be here with me, and those adorable boys you're obsessed with wouldn't be living their last day."

Hayley's stomach lurched at his words. She considered punching his face, wondering if the results would be anything other than him knocking her out in retaliation. "Your friend?" she snapped instead. "You mean the gunman who shot into a crowd? Probably the same one who performed that drive-by at the Everetts' house and blew up the warehouse."

Forrester shrugged. "Ever heard the expression 'you've got to do what you've got to do'?"

She curled her hands into fists on her lap. "People were shot today. Maybe killed. All so you could build some bougie condos? Get away with another murder? What is wrong with you?"

"Nothing I can't fix," he said.

She dragged her gaze over the familiar buildings of the waterfront. Broken and dilapidated. Uninhabited and unsafe. Tagged and spray-painted by lost souls and street artists. Like Gage.

Memories of the explosion that had nearly killed her and Finn crashed through her mind. The hissing stick of explosives from a nearby demolition site that sent them into the water. Her body shuddered in response. Their survival had been miraculous, but now she was back on the same block. Alone with a madman.

Signs with the Lighthouse, Inc. logo flapped and fluttered in the growing wind. The relentless sun was blocked by gray clouds of a brewing storm.

"All of this trash and rubble will soon be gone," he said, slowing outside a building surrounded by a chain-link fence. "I'm making sure of it. One building at a time." He parked and climbed out, then pointed his handgun through the open window at Hayley. "Come on. I've got somewhere to be."

She eased onto her feet, scanning the vacant streets, and holding on to his last few words. If he didn't plan to kill her immediately, she'd soon be left alone. And she could be incredibly resourceful. She wouldn't have survived her childhood otherwise.

The building behind the fence was tall and newer than most in the area. "Are the boys in there?" she asked.

"One way to find out," Forrester said, rounding the hood. He grabbed her by the arm and jerked, causing her to stumble.

Then he towed her onto the sidewalk and through an unlocked gate. No Trespassing signs warned that unauthorized visitors would be prosecuted. Other signage announced the property's scheduled demolition. Goose bumps tightened her skin as she read the date.

Tomorrow morning.

"The good news is you'll only be spending one night here," Forester said, tugging her along more quickly as they approached the entryway. "The whole place will be dust tomorrow, along with everything in it."

Her eyes strained for focus as she stepped inside. The loss of sunlight left her temporarily without sight. The space was silent. No indication they weren't alone. Were the boys really there? Or had she been duped? Believed the lie, and gone willfully to her death?

Forester led her down a hallway as her vision cleared. Then he paused outside a sturdy-looking interior door. He pulled a key from his pocket and freed a padlock from a heavy chain. He swung the barrier open to reveal a dark set of steps to the basement. "In you go."

Before she could protest or make a plan to run, the sound of his cocking gun clicked beside her ear.

"You don't want the kid to see another woman murdered, do you?"

She took a step into the darkness, and Forester gave her a heavy shove. Hayley screamed as she fell forward, clutching the handrail and pressing her body to the wall for stability. Her feet fumbled down several steps to a landing, before she crashed onto her hands and knees with a thud.

The door slammed shut behind her, and the rattle of chains being secured forced a sob from her throat. Suffocating heat covered her like a blanket. Sweat broke instantly above her lip and across her brow. There were a few more steps to navigate before she reached the sublevel and whatever awaited her down there.

Soft shuffling sounds sent her onto her feet, back pressed to the wall. "Who's there?"

A pinhole of light appeared, and the space became

faintly visible. The room was lined with empty shelving. Maybe previously used for storage. A small window near an exposed-beam ceiling had been painted black and lined with bars.

"Hayley?" Gage's voice reached to her. The sound was thin and weak.

"Gage!" She rushed in the direction of the sound, down the final steps and around an overturned table near the light. Two filthy figures were huddled on the ground. "Parker." She gathered the boys into her arms and held them tight.

Gage winced and hissed.

She released them with a jolt of fear. "What's wrong?"

"He's hurt," Parker said. "He tried to get us out of here, but he fell."

"Fell?"

Parker pointed to the window high above.

"I think my arm's broken," Gage said. "This is all my fault. I shouldn't have been down here that night. I should've told you what I saw the next day."

Hayley squinted at his arm, cradled to his torso, scraped and bruised. "It's okay," she assured him. "Everyone understands why you ran and why you hid. No one blames you. No one's mad. I'm just so glad you're okay. We're going to get out of here, take you to a hospital and go home with the coolest cast you've ever seen. Okay?"

Gage nodded, but neither he nor Parker looked as if they believed her.

She refreshed her smile. "The good news is that the police are looking for you. They'll be looking for me now too."

"What about me?" Parker asked, his small voice ripping a fresh hole in Hayley's heart.

"They know the two of you are together," she said, stroking a hand over his hair. "We've all been very worried."

"I shouldn't have taken him," Gage said. "I knew he was scared, and I thought I could help. The Michaelsons were bad people. The next family might've been worse."

"No." She set a palm against his cheek. "The Michaelsons are the exception, not the rule. I'm so sorry no one realized sooner. Most foster families are wonderful and kind. Thanks to you guys, no children will ever be placed in that family's care again. I think that makes you heroes."

Parker beamed.

Gage snorted. "What kind of hero gets a woman and a little boy killed? Did you see the signs outside?"

Hayley nodded at Gage. "We can't wait around to be rescued. We're going to have to find a way out by ourselves." She scanned the boys in the little shaft of light.

Had they eaten since being brought here? Had they been given any water? Gage grimaced with each little movement, clearly in terrible pain.

"What were you doing when you fell?" she asked him. "What was your plan for escape?"

"I thought I could break the glass behind those bars and call for help, but I slipped and fell."

"What were you going to break the glass with?"

He lifted his uninjured arm to reveal bruised and bloody knuckles. "It's glass block under the paint. It's not breaking."

Parker burrowed closer to Gage, fitting himself against the older boy's side and winding thin arms around his torso.

"It's okay," Gage whispered. "I'm right here, and I've got you."

Hayley rose and walked the room's perimeter, evaluating the situation and attempting to clear her head. Her eyes returned to the pinhole of light, the result of a small hole in the exterior wall.

"We were staying at the art studio where my dad taught classes," Gage said. "We were going to be okay. I don't know how they found us."

"I was thirsty," Parker said. "It was my fault. I asked to go to the store again."

"It's not your fault, buddy," Gage soothed.

"He's right," Hayley said. "The only person at fault for this is the man who brought us here." She approached the shelves at the far wall, reaching a hand overhead and searching for something she could use as a weapon if needed.

"He caught us before we made it back to the studio," Gage said. "We tried to run, but—" His heartbroken expression said Parker was too small to outrun a grown man, and too big for Gage to carry.

She nodded. "You haven't done anything wrong. Neither of you. Right now, we have to think about how to get out of here. We can sort the rest later."

"The window is the only way," Gage said. "The door's bolted and chained."

"But the wall is weak," she said, pointing to the pinhole of light. "That brick is already crumbling. Any idea where we can find something to make that hole bigger?" she asked. "Maybe big enough for us to climb out?"

Parker's eyes widened. "That would have to be a lot bigger."

Gage pushed onto his feet with a sharp intake of air. He offered his hand to Parker, pulling him up beside him. Then he limped across the space to her side, left arm cradled across his middle. Apparently, he'd hurt his leg or ankle too. "Let's help Hayley get us out of here."

A few minutes later, they'd found an old piece of rebar, a few large nails and the broken handle of a tool Hayley couldn't name. She'd hoped for a forgotten sledgehammer, but she was willing to make do with anything that would save the lives of these boys.

"All right," she said. "Let's see what we can do about that escape."

Together, they attacked the bricks near the light, working steadily for what felt like an eternity in the heat, until the light outside began to dim. Distant sounds of thunder rumbled in the sky.

The boys stopped to rest, both saying they felt dizzy and weak.

Gage curled into a ball and heaved.

Parker cried.

Hayley offered soothing words and sat with them until they fell asleep. Then she got back to work. Tomorrow, the building was coming down. Today was all they had left and it was nearing an end.

Brick by busted brick, she had to get them out of there.

Chapter Twenty-One

Finn paced his small office inside the Marshal's Bluff police station, a cell phone pressed to his ear. Beyond the open door, his team sifted through reports from witnesses at the press-conference shooting. Thankfully there hadn't been any fatalities and only a handful of minor injuries. Unfortunately, no one had noticed Hayley leaving, but she'd been gone when he returned.

He never should've left her alone.

A soft knock sounded and Dean appeared. He waved from the threshold. "Any luck?"

Finn rubbed a heavy palm against his forehead then anchored the hand against the back of his neck. It'd been hours since the most recent shooting, and none of the resulting leads had panned out. The gunman had yet to be identified, and Hayley had become vapor. "I'm on hold with Tech Services," he said. "Someone called the tip line after we aired that piece on the news about Hayley's disappearance. The caller claimed to have been eating at an outdoor café when a dark sedan stopped at the light on the corner in the shopping district. A woman fitting Hayley's description was in the passenger seat. The caller didn't get a look at the driver and couldn't say whether or not the woman appeared upset or injured, but it's the only somewhat solid lead we've got.

Tech Services used the time and location to pull a partial plate from the car. They're running the number now." He motioned Dean inside. "What about you? Anything new?"

"Maybe," Dean said, stepping into the office and leaning against the wall beside the door. "I visited the country club where the Everetts and Forester are members."

"Yeah?" Finn asked. He'd been meaning to get to the country club for days but hadn't managed. "What'd you learn?"

"According to the bartender I spoke with, the Everetts were friends with Forester until suddenly they weren't."

Finn stilled. "Keep going."

Dean shrugged. "She didn't know why, only that there's a weekly poker tournament held after hours at the club. It's an invitation-only situation and only the wealthiest are invited. Lots of money exchanges hands, and big business deals are made, but no one talks about it on the record."

Finn sighed. "But the bartender knew and shared the details with you."

"She knew because she gets paid in tips to work the events," Dean said. "She shared because rumor has it I'm charming."

Finn sighed. "Go on."

Dean grinned. "Guess who lost a lot of money to Conrad Forester last month?"

"Tell me it was Kate Everett's husband."

Dean nodded. "I don't have specifics or proof, but that was the story making the rounds at the end of the night."

"Okay." Finn's mind raced with fresh theories. "So Everett owed Forrester. Any idea how much?"

"No, but they allegedly agreed to call it even if Everett got his wife to change the location of her community-center project." Dean's eyebrows raised and he crossed his arms over his chest, looking rightfully proud.

"Detective Beaumont?" The voice of the tech-services representative rang in his ear.

He'd temporarily forgotten about the phone in his hand. "Yeah, I'm here."

"Plates on that sedan match a vehicle registered to Conrad Forester. Would you like the home address and phone number on file?"

"Text it," Finn said, already headed into the hall to collect his team.

FINN NAVIGATED THE streets of Old Downtown, his heart in his throat and a storm rolling in off the coast. Forester hadn't been at his home or office, but Mr. Everett had started talking the moment Finn and Dean showed up at his door. He confessed his debt to Forester and explained that Kate had refused to change her dream over a game of poker.

Finn was willing to bet Forester hadn't liked that answer.

Now Dean was riding shotgun in Finn's borrowed SUV, the team close behind.

Forester owned enough properties along the waterfront to keep them all busy past nightfall, but it was the perfect place to hide two kids and a woman, so they wouldn't stop until they'd searched every square foot.

"So Everett owes Forester a gambling debt he can't pay up," Dean said, verbally sorting the facts. "At first he can't pay, because his wife controls the business and the money. Then Forester kills the wife, or has her killed, to stop the project, but Everett still doesn't control the business."

"He told me a board of trustees was handling things now," Finn said. "I'm unclear about his access or control of the money."

Lightning flashed as he parked the SUV on the street where it had all began. Three other vehicles followed suit, and his teammates filed onto the sidewalk. One side of the street contained the warehouse remains. Across the broken asphalt, yellow crime-scene tape denoted the location of Kate's murder. All around, signs with the Lighthouse, Inc. logo were pelted with falling rain.

Finn's phone dinged, and he paused to check the screen.

"News?" Dean asked, unfastening his safety belt.

"The lab," Finn said, scanning the message. "Bullet casings found after the press-conference shooting match those pulled from my truck after the drive-by and the one in Kate's body."

The same weapon had been used in all three crime scenes.

"And the case just gets stronger," Dean said.

Finn released a labored sigh. "Against Lance Stevens. We probably have enough to arrest him for the shootings and murder, but we'll need to prove Forester's connection to him and those crimes."

"So first we'll find Hayley," Dean said, opening his door against the increasing wind. "I have a feeling she's all we'll need to arrest him for abduction. And as soon as you do your cop thing and offer Stevens a deal, I'm sure he'll roll on Forester for hiring him as the gunman."

Lightning flashed in the sky, and Finn stepped into the storm. He'd bring Hayley home safely, whatever the cost.

HAYLEY WHIMPERED AS thunder rolled and she worked her bloody fingers over broken bricks, painstakingly tearing them free. Her hands were filthy and swollen from the work. Her arms and chest were covered in dust and dirt from the aged mortar and crumbling masonry. Tears streamed over her red-hot cheeks, and icy fear coiled in her gut. Her voice was nearly gone from continuous and desperate cries for help.

The boys rested on the floor, dehydrated and exhausted.

Gage's pain had increased by the minute as he'd beaten the rebar against the wall, each whack reverberating through his thin frame and jostling his broken arm.

She was making progress on her own, but it was too slow to expect an escape before dawn. Even if she worked all night. The hole was large enough to get her foot through, but nothing more.

She swallowed a scream of rage at the unfairness of it all and reached again for the rebar. Her sweaty, blood-slicked hands slipped as she swung, tearing the skin of her palms and raising fire in her veins. "Dammit!"

Outside the foot-size hole, rain soaked the ground, creating mini rivers and mudslides that slopped over the brick wall and onto the basement floor. The rain would prevent any passersby close enough to hear her screams. If not, the thunder would surely cover the feeble sound.

She swung her weapon harder, funneling all the hate and fear inside her into each new swing. Every jarring thud wrenched a fresh sob from her chest until she couldn't lift the metal or her arms.

"Ms. Hayley?" Parker asked, wobbling onto his feet, fear in his wide brown eyes.

She wiped her face and forced her mind into caregiver mode. Their situation was dire, but Parker was only eight, and he needed her protection.

Before she could find the words to speak, a great, rolling groan spread through the structure above them. The wall she'd been assaulting began to shift, and the bricks began to fall. Dirt dropped onto their heads from the exposed ceiling beams and joists.

Gage pressed onto his feet with a sharp wince of pain. "What's happening?"

Hayley's heart seized in horrific realization as she watched broken bits of brick and mortar spill from the wall. Her failed attempt to save them would be the death of them instead.

She'd intentionally damaged a load-bearing wall.

"The building is unstable," she said, as calmly as she could manage.

Gage nodded in grim understanding. "What do we do?"

Parker peered through the growing hole. "Boost me up! I can fit!"

Hayley dragged her gaze from Parker to the opening as thunder boomed and lightning struck.

Sending Parker alone into the most dangerous area of town, into the storm and darkness, wasn't an answer she'd ever choose. But her choices had been erased.

Gage stepped into the space at her side. "Help," he instructed. "I can't lift him on my own. Parker, keep running until you find someone to tell we're down here. Then ask to call 911. Watch out for the man who brought us here. Look for his car. Be careful."

Parker raised a thumb, his attention fixed on the small opening in the wall. "Got it," he said. "I'm a hero."

"That's right," Gage said. "You're a hero. And, hey, don't come back here without an adult, understand? No matter what happens. Even if this building makes a lot of noise. Stay focused. Okay?"

Hayley swallowed a rock of emotion as she processed Gage's words of protection. If the building fell, Parker couldn't come back alone. Couldn't try to save them. Couldn't be hurt or worse by the unstable ruins. Whatever else happened, Parker would survive.

She helped Gage hoist the little boy into the storm.

Chapter Twenty-Two

Hayley swung the rebar at the shelving on the walls, dismantling it with every bone-rattling blow. "Gage, take these," she said, kicking boards and sections of fallen framework across the floor in the teen's direction. "Wedge them in the opening. Use them to support the wall."

A few busted shelves wouldn't stop a building from collapsing, but she could at least try to buy them some time. Give the miracle they desperately needed a chance to happen.

Gage had already been abducted and injured on her watch. She couldn't sit idly by and wait for them both to be crushed to death.

His face contorted in pain as he tried to place the boards between broken bricks.

"Let me help," she said, abandoning the demolition to assist in the new project. "Go ahead and rest. I've got this."

Gage stepped away, breathing heavily and pressing his broken arm to his torso.

Hayley stayed on task, working the boards into place between rows of still-sturdy bricks. The gap had grown exponentially with each ugly groan of the building, and a new realization hit with the next boom of thunder. "I think you can fit through this."

"What?" Gage returned to her side with a frown.

"Look!"

He squinted at the hole she'd braced, and a low cuss rolled off his tongue. "Sorry."

"Darling, I'm going to agree," she said. "Here." Gusts of cool, wet air blew into the basement as she laced her fingers together and formed a stirrup for his foot. "I'll give you a boost."

"What about you?" he asked, unmoving. "There's no one to boost you out if I leave. You'll still be stuck down here."

"I'll figure it out," she said. "Don't worry about me. You need to go look for help."

"I won't leave you."

The battering wind picked up, and the building moaned. Dirt fell in tufts from the space above their heads. Time was running out.

She needed to get Gage as far away as possible. Fast.

"I can climb out," she said. "I still have two good arms and legs. You're limping." She crouched and wiggled her joined hands. "Come on. Hurry."

Gage scanned her face, distrusting.

"Let's go," she urged. "The quicker you get out there, the sooner I can too."

Reluctantly, he set a foot onto her hands, and a tear rolled over his cheek. "You'd better make it out. I'm trusting you," he whispered.

She nodded, then she shoved him into the night.

FINN AND DEAN crossed the first floor of the third empty building they'd painstakingly cleared. There were dozens more and not enough law enforcement in the county to search them all in a short amount of time. "Maybe we need to arrange search parties," Finn said.

"We're not even sure they're in Old Downtown," Dean

countered. "Lighthouse, Inc. owns a lot of properties in this area."

"We'd know sooner if we had more boots on the ground."

"Help!" The word seemed to echo in the storm.

Finn stilled, senses on high alert. "Did you hear that?" He focused on the sound, praying it would come again.

Dean raised his flashlight beam toward the open door ahead. "What?"

"It came from outside," Finn said, rushing through the building and onto the sidewalk.

In the distance, a small figure ran along a parallel street. "Help!"

"Hey!" Finn barked, projecting his most authoritative tone and hoping he would be heard.

The boy stopped and turned, then launched in their direction, arms waving. "Help! Help! Help!"

"Parker?" Finn met him in the intersection, pulling him into his arms. "Where did you come from? Are Hayley and Gage with you?"

Parker nodded. "They're in the basement. Gage is hurt."

"Okay, buddy." Finn said. "This is my brother Dean and he's going to get you out of the rain." Finn turned to pass Parker into Dean's arms.

"No! We have to help them!" Parker cried. "The building is getting blown up tomorrow. They didn't think I saw the signs, but I did, and I can read. I'm a very good reader."

Finn's chest constricted and his gaze whipped from building to building. "Which one?"

Parker scanned the street, wiping water from his terror-filled eyes. "We made a hole in the wall, and it started to fall apart."

"Which building?" Finn repeated, more harshly than intended, earning a stern look from Dean.

Dean pried the child from his arms. "Get your team out here," he told Finn. "We've got to be close."

Finn dialed his team and relayed the information while Dean ducked under a nearby awning with Parker.

Finn followed.

"You're okay," Dean said gently. "We're going to keep you safe and help the others. Can you show us where you were?"

Parker wound narrow arms around Dean's neck and whimpered. "I don't know."

"Do you remember which way you ran?"

Parker shook his head.

"What can you remember?" Finn asked, careful not to upset the kid further. "You said there were signs?"

"And a fence," Parker said.

"That's good," Dean encouraged. "Anything else?"

Parker buried his face against Dean's neck.

Finn patted the boy's back. "You did great, buddy. We'll take it from here, and you can get dry." He waved a hand at his teammates as they filtered out of nearby buildings, converged, then rushed to his aid.

Dean passed Parker into another set of hands.

"We need ambulances and the search-and-rescue team down here," Finn instructed. "Have him checked out and kept under guard." He nodded at Parker. "Don't let him out of your sight. We also need a list of buildings set for demolition in the morning. We're looking for one with a fence."

The group split up, and Finn caught his brother's eye. "SUV."

They both broke into a sprint for the vehicle they'd left behind. Within seconds, they were onboard and in motion.

Finn pressed the gas pedal with purpose, hydroplaning over the flooding roads.

"There are a few buildings behind fences at the end of

the next block," Dean said. "I saw them the day of the warehouse explosion. I was looking for construction locations that might have explosives on-site."

Finn adjusted his wipers and heat vents, attempting to clear his view. Sheets of rain washed over the windshield, and storm clouds had turned dusk to night.

He leaned forward, peering over his steering wheel and straining for visibility. A moment later, he slowed, confusion mixing with hope. "I think I see someone out there." He veered to the road's flooded edge, sending a mini tidal wave across the sidewalk.

A narrow figure weaved in their direction, cradling one arm, head bent low against the wind and rain.

The Beaumonts jumped out and ran in the figure's direction.

"Gage?" Finn called. Could his luck truly be so good? To find not one, but both missing boys, in the middle of this storm?

The teen raised his head, stopping several feet away. "Finn!" he cried. "Help!" He swung an arm to point in the opposite direction. "Hayley's still inside, and the building's coming down!"

"We know," Finn said, erasing the final steps between them and projecting his voice against the wind. "Parker's with my team. He told us about the demolition tomorrow."

"No!" Gage turned back, eyes wild. "We broke a load-bearing wall and—"

Finn's ears rang as he raised his eyes to the silhouettes of distant structures.

And in the next breath, a building began to fall.

HAYLEY DRAGGED THE remnants of a broken shelving unit to the collapsing wall and climbed on to test its strength.

Overhead, the building's complaints grew more fervent with every powerful gust of wind. She stretched onto tiptoe, reaching through the hole in search of purchase. There wasn't anyone left to offer her a boost. No one to grab her hands and pull her up. She'd demanded that Gage leave her and find Parker, then bring help.

She pressed the toe of one shoe into a crevice between bricks and thrust her torso outside with a harsh shove. The busted shelving crashed onto the floor, leaving her half inside and half out. The ground was slippery and soft from the storm. Each wiggle and stretch toward freedom threatened to land her back where she'd started.

If she died, two young boys would carry a lifetime of guilt with them for leaving her behind, and she would not allow that to happen.

Slowly, she got to her knees then pushed onto her feet.

She pulled in a shaky breath, stunned and elated to know she'd won. She'd gotten the boys to safety, and she'd beaten Forester at his twisted game.

A horrendous cracking sound filled the night and set her in motion toward the chain-link fence. She ran faster than she'd thought possible as the building came down behind her.

Hunks of busted bricks bounced and rolled over the sopping ground, crashing against her feet and legs. She stumbled and fell. Her body screamed with pain, and her forehead collided with the walkway. Then the world went dark…

Hayley. Her name echoed in her ears, sounding foreign, fuzzy. Her eyes reopened, mind aware of what she'd been through.

Rain had soaked and added weight to her clothes. Lightning flashed in the sky above.

"Hayley!"

She rolled onto her back, head pounding and heart racing as the remains of the building she'd escaped from came into view. Half of the massive structure was gone, revealing the insides, like a giant, ghastly dollhouse.

Emergency sirens warbled in the distance, and the glow of searchlights danced over the rubble around her. She'd survived, and she was being rescued.

"There she is!" a male voice called. "Beaumont! I see her!"

Hayley twisted on the ground, seeking the man behind the name. She pushed up, onto skinned knees, then to her feet. Searching.

"Hayley," Finn said, striding through the storm like her personal hero. He moved faster and with purpose as their eyes met, erasing the distance between them until she was in his arms.

SIX MONTHS LATER, the summer heat had gone, but Hayley's nights were just as hot, and her days were filled with warmth and light. Today was no different.

Conrad Forester was in jail for conspiracy to commit murder, multiple counts of attempted murder and abduction, extortion, plus a whole host of other crimes. Most of which he'd readily admitted to in the hopes of a plea bargain. But a loose-lipped gunman and a rock-solid case by Finn and the Marshal's Bluff PD had put him away for life instead.

Katherine Everett's community-center project was well underway, and her husband was fully involved in making it everything she'd hoped.

Hayley had been promoted to a position for the routine reevaluation of foster families. And the job came with less overtime. All in all, it had been a pretty terrific six months.

She smiled as Finn parked the truck outside his parents'

home and glanced over his shoulder at the boys in the extended cab.

"You guys ready?" he asked.

"Yeah!" Parker called.

Gage rolled his eyes.

Hayley turned and smiled at the pair.

If anyone had told her last summer that she'd be married with two children before the holidays, she'd have told them they had the wrong woman. If they'd told her the children would be eight and fourteen years old, she'd have assumed they were off their rockers. But adopting Gage and Parker was the best, smartest, most wonderful thing she'd ever done.

Marrying the love of her life a few months prior was a possible tie.

Finn climbed out, then opened the rear door and grinned. "I can't wait to see everyone's face when they hear the news."

A mass of Beaumonts spilled onto the porch before Hayley made it to the steps. Gage trailed a short distance behind, carrying a neatly wrapped box.

"Grandma!" Parker said, running to Mrs. Beaumont's arms.

She kissed his head and tousled his hair with a smile. "What's this about exciting news?"

Austin, Dean and Lincoln moved to stand beside their dad.

Nicole, Dean's fiancée, and Scarlet, Austin's new wife, closed in on Hayley.

Josi brought up the rear. "Please tell me there's going to be a baby."

Hayley turned a bright smile on Finn. "Not yet."

He pulled Gage against his side. "We'd like to get this one into college first."

"So what's the news?" Austin asked. "It's freezing, and Mom said you wanted us all outside."

Hayley traded knowing looks with her family. "We aren't having a baby, but our family is growing."

Gage raised the box in his hands, and Parker whipped off the lid.

"We got a puppy!" Parker yelled, buzzing with the same excitement he'd had since Finn and Hayley had taken the boys to select their new pet.

"He's a hound dog," Gage said proudly. "He howls. It's hilarious."

Hayley wound an arm around his back, forming a chain with Gage and Finn, while the others oohed and aahed over Parker and the puppy.

"His name is Sir Barks-a-lot," Parker announced.

"I'm not calling him that," Lincoln said, swinging Parker under one arm like a football.

Josi cuddled the pup to her chest. "I think it's cute."

"I think it's cold," Austin complained, dragging Scarlet in for a hug. "Bring that little furball inside. Parker can come too."

"Hey!" Parker laughed.

The group filed into Mrs. Beaumont's kitchen, but Hayley and Finn stayed behind.

Gage shook his head and laughed, but shut the door in his wake…leaving them to do the thing they spent an awful lot of time doing these days.

Kissing and savoring the moments.

* * * * *

Don't miss the final book in Julie Anne Lindsey's
Beaumont Brothers Justice miniseries,
Under Siege,
on sale next month!

And look for the other books in the series:

Closing In On Clues
Always Watching

Available now from Harlequin Intrigue!